princess

Belinda Ray

SCHOLASTIC INC.
New York Toronto London Auckland Sydney
Mexico City New Delhi Hong Kong Buenos Aires

For Ian and Evan, who are always my first readers
—B.R.

ISBN 0-439-67635-5

Published by Scholastic Inc.

Produced by 17th Street Productions,
an Alloy company
151 West 26th Street
New York, NY 10001

12 11 10 9 8 7 6 5 4 7 8 9/0

Printed in the U.S.A. 40
First printing, November 2004

princess

CHAPTER One

Jasmine wiped away a small circle of condensation from the passenger side window and peered through it. What she saw nearly took her breath away.

"You can just drop me here, Mom," she blurted.

Her mother was about to drive around the drop-off circle at Elizabeth Cady Stanton Middle School, but she slowed to a stop instead. "Are you sure?" she asked, glancing at her daughter. "The main entrance is up ahead."

"I'm sure," Jasmine replied, her eyes on the two girls she'd spotted standing in the courtyard at the side of the building. Plenty of students were milling about there, but the two girls nearest the road were the ones who had caught her attention.

"All right," Mrs. Porter said with a shrug.

She leaned toward Jasmine, giving her a quick peck on the cheek. "I'll stop at the office to make sure your registration is all set. Do you have everything—notebooks, lunch money, gym clothes?"

Jasmine sighed. "Yes, Mom," she droned, and before her mother could catch her in a sentimental it's-your-first-day-at-your-new-school embrace, Jasmine pushed open the door and hopped out.

"See you at three," her mother called.

"Uh-huh," Jasmine mumbled, her attention on the brick building before her and the two girls she'd seen from the car. They were standing with their backs to her, about thirty feet away. One of them had curly red hair and the other had long brown hair in cornrows spilling down her back. They were taller than Jasmine remembered them, and their hair was styled differently, but still—it had to be them: Carrie Weingarten and Theresa Allen.

Jasmine began to walk toward the courtyard, wondering if they would recognize her—or if they would even remember her. It had been nearly two years since the last time she'd seen them. That was when Mrs. Porter had gotten a new job in Boston and she and Jasmine had relocated midyear. *Two years is a long time,*

Jasmine thought. In that time, she'd changed a lot.

In third grade, she'd loved oldies music. Now she was into techno. Her favorite subject then had been math, but now she loved art. Her once-long brown hair was now cropped short, she'd grown about four inches, and while she'd always been a trendy dresser, she'd definitely stepped it up a level. Lately she'd even been making some of her own clothes and creating new trends. But surely, even with all those changes, Carrie and Theresa would still recognize her, right? After all, they'd been her best friends.

Jasmine took a deep breath. The two girls were talking and laughing, and Jasmine was on the verge of calling out to them when a disturbing thought stopped her in her tracks. What if they recognized her right away, but for some reason they didn't like her anymore? Sure, they'd been friends two years ago, but that didn't mean they could automatically pick up where they left off. Jasmine gulped.

Maybe she, Carrie, and Theresa no longer had anything in common. Jasmine's heart sped up, and suddenly walking right over to her old friends didn't seem like such a great idea. She was contemplating what to do when a voice nearby startled her.

"Jasmine? Jasmine Porter? Is that you?"

Jasmine had been so preoccupied with her former friends that she hadn't noticed the approaching girl, and when she realized who it was, she wished she had run right up to Carrie and Theresa without hesitating. Even if they had completely ignored her, it would have been a better start to her day than meeting up with Ashley Dutton. Jasmine was caught so off guard that all she could do was stare.

"What's wrong? Don't you remember me?" the girl said with a slight sneer.

Jasmine blinked once, slowly. "Ashley," she said evenly. "How could I forget?"

The sixth grader smirked, her big blue eyes wide with excitement. "Is that any way to greet an old friend?" she asked.

"An old friend?" Jasmine echoed. "Are you joking?" She glanced over Ashley's shoulder at Carrie and Theresa, who still hadn't noticed her. *They* were old friends. Ashley was, if anything, an old enemy.

Back in third grade, Ashley had taken every possible opportunity to humiliate Jasmine, all because Ashley's crush, Kirk Goldsberry, had declared one day that he thought Jasmine was the prettiest girl in the school. From that moment on, Ashley had set out to make Jasmine's life miserable.

She made fun of Jasmine's clothes, her hair, the way she walked, the way she talked, the car her mother drove—anything she could think of—until the teasing became a regular part of Jasmine's school day, just like homeroom, lunch, and recess. And apparently, despite Jasmine's twenty-three-month absence from Newcastle, Ashley still hadn't managed to kick the habit.

Her eyes traveled slowly down to Jasmine's feet and back up to her face. "Did you get dressed in a circus tent this morning, or are those your real clothes?" she asked.

Jasmine looked down at her outfit and then glanced around the school yard. Nearly everyone else was wearing jeans and simple cotton tees or some variation of that basic outfit. Even Ashley, who had always been a pretty trendy dresser, was wearing plain light-blue capri pants and a pale blue-and-white-striped boatneck sweater with flip-flops. It was cute but conservative, and Ashley blended well with the rest of the crowd. Jasmine, on the other hand, stood out like a canary in a group of penguins.

What was I thinking? Jasmine wondered, surveying her outfit one more time. Black lace-up boots with chunky soles, bright yellow tights, a zebra-print skirt, a black tank with a ruffle down the front, and a beat-up, secondhand, green wool cardigan. She'd even twisted her hair into a funky bun and secured it with cheetah-patterned hair sticks. She would have been less conspicuous balancing a pelican on her head and riding a unicycle.

"I—um," Jasmine said after a moment. They were the only words she could manage. She felt like she was in one of those dreams where she'd gone to school in her pajamas, only she knew that there was no waking up from this nightmare.

"Wow. Nice comeback," Ashley jeered. "Did you think—" she started, but she was interrupted by a blaring car horn from behind.

"Have a good day, Jazzy!" Mrs. Porter yelled as she drove by in her old station wagon. Jasmine watched as her mother continued up the drive, laying on the horn two more times and waving frantically.

Oh, man, Jasmine thought. *As if things weren't bad enough already.* Everyone in the courtyard was probably pointing at her and laughing now. *Thanks, Mom,* Jasmine thought bitterly, but before she even got a chance to check Ashley's reaction—or anyone else's—she found herself being practically tackled by a girl with a mass of curly red hair and another girl with gleaming white teeth.

"Theresa! Carrie!" Jasmine cried, throwing her arms around her old friends. "It's so awesome to see you guys!"

"You too, Jazzy!" the girls replied, grinning and laughing.

"How sweet," Ashley jeered. "A geek reunion."

The three girls stopped giggling and turned toward Ashley, and for the first time, Jasmine noticed that a fourth girl had joined them—a small girl with straight black hair and shiny dark eyes. She was wearing jeans and a white peasant blouse with little red flowers around the neckline. Nice, but still pretty conservative. She probably came over to help Ashley make fun of Jasmine's crazy outfit.

"So, anyway," Ashley went on with an unpleasant grin, "I was just admiring Jasmine's . . . *clothing choices.*"

Jasmine felt her entire body grow hot with embarrassment. She had hoped that Ashley would lay off now that Carrie and Theresa were there to back her up, but Ashley didn't seem to care who heard her.

Even worse, Jasmine noticed that Carrie and Theresa were now eyeing her from head to toe.

Judging from their simple sweaters, jeans, and nearly identical slip-on sneakers, Jasmine was sure they thought she was just as weird as Ashley did.

"Where did you get that outfit anyway, Jasmine? Dorks R Us?" Ashley asked, smirking.

Jasmine saw Theresa wince, and Carrie glanced at the ground, her face turning pink. *They're embarrassed by me!* Jasmine thought, cringing. Why hadn't she worn something more subdued on her first day of school? All she wanted to do was crawl under a rock and disappear, but she couldn't even bring herself to move.

The silence had grown almost unbearable when suddenly the small girl with the black hair spoke. "Wow, what a coincidence, Ashley," she said in a serious tone. "You know, I was just about to ask you if that's where you got your personality."

Jasmine's eyebrows shot up, but Ashley scowled. "Who are you?" she spat.

"My name is Anna," the small girl said with a bright smile. "I just moved here a little while ago, and I have to say, it's *so* good to meet you."

Jasmine wasn't sure what to make of this girl, and apparently Ashley wasn't, either. Her features softened a bit, but she stared at the girl—*Anna*—cautiously. "Really?" she asked.

"Absolutely," Anna said. "I was starting to get a little freaked out at how *nice* everyone here is. It's good to see that there's at least *one* really nasty person in this school."

Jasmine gasped. She'd never heard anyone speak to Ashley like that before. She glanced at Theresa and Carrie and saw that while they still looked a bit uncomfortable, they had both begun to giggle.

Ashley squinted at Anna for a moment, then flipped her blond hair over her shoulder indignantly and turned back to Jasmine with a smirk. "Anyway," she said, "I just wanted to say hi and tell you how much I like your . . . *outfit.*" As she finished the sentence, she burst out laughing, and so did a group of her friends who were watching a short distance away. Jasmine hadn't noticed them before, but they'd obviously been listening—and snickering at Jasmine—the whole time.

"Don't let her bother you, Jasmine," Carrie said when Ashley was gone.

Jasmine looked up at her. "It's kind of hard not to," she said. "Is she still as popular as she used to be?" Theresa and Carrie avoided meeting Jasmine's eyes, but they both nodded. "Shoot," Jasmine said with a sigh. "She's going to start picking on me all over again, isn't she?"

Carried shrugged.

"Maybe not," said Theresa, but she didn't sound hopeful.

"Not if you stand up to her," said the small girl with the black hair. Jasmine stared at her with narrowed eyes. Who *was* this girl, anyway?

"Oh—I'm sorry," Carrie said, looking from Jasmine to the girl and back again. "Jasmine, this is Anna Lee. She just moved here from California."

"A couple of months ago," Theresa added, "but it feels like she's been here forever."

Anna scrunched her eyebrows together. "Is that a compliment, or are you saying that you're sick of me?"

"No way," Carrie replied, swatting Anna's arm playfully. "We love having you here. And Jasmine, you're going to love Anna, too. She's great at putting people in their place."

"Yeah, I guess so," Jasmine said, glancing toward Ashley and her group of friends. "Thanks," she added, turning back to Anna.

"No problem," Anna said. "Who does that girl think she is, anyway?"

"One of the most popular people in school," Jasmine said.

"Well, that doesn't give her the right to be

rude," Anna said. "If she says anything else, you should offer to pay for her next attitude adjustment—she obviously needs one."

Jasmine chuckled in spite of herself. Anna was definitely quick, and funny, too. Unfortunately, Jasmine didn't share her talent. She knew she'd never be able to say anything about attitude adjustments to Ashley or anyone else. Sassy comebacks weren't exactly her strength.

"Besides, I don't know what she was talking about," Anna went on. "I really like your outfit."

"Me, too," Carrie piped up immediately.

"Ditto," Theresa agreed.

Jasmine surveyed the three girls. They were all smiling at her enthusiastically, but she couldn't help thinking that they were just trying to make her feel better. "Thanks," she murmured, scuffing the toe of her left boot against the pavement and watching a pebble go skittering away.

"Hey—do you want to go see your new homeroom?" Carrie asked.

Jasmine nodded. She'd have gone to watch paint dry if it meant getting away from Ashley Dutton and out of the crowded courtyard. She was beginning to catch stares and grins from other students now—more every second, it seemed. Of course, the loudest giggles were still coming from Ashley's crew, but others were definitely joining in.

As the four girls crossed the courtyard, Jasmine pulled her cardigan tight around her body. She wasn't cold, but with all the looks she was getting, she felt a need to cover up as much as possible. And once they were inside, Jasmine ducked into the first bathroom she could find.

In the safety of a stall, she pulled off her tights and threw them into her backpack. It would be a little chilly, but bare legs were definitely less noticeable than bright yellow ones. Next she turned her zebra skirt inside out so that the black lining showed instead of the bold print. And finally, she buttoned the cardigan all the way up in front to hide her ruffley tank.

There, she thought, checking herself in the mirror above the sink. *A plain black skirt and a sweater—much more Newcastle, New Hampshire.* There was nothing she could do about the boots, but hopefully with the rest of her outfit toned down, they wouldn't stand out quite so much.

When she came out of the bathroom, her three friends were waiting for her, and they all eyed her suspiciously.

"You changed?" Theresa asked, confused.

Jasmine pretended to be surprised by the question. "Huh? Oh—yeah. I, um, spilled soap on myself when I was washing my hands, so I just turned my skirt inside out."

"What about your tights?" Carrie asked.

"They're in my backpack," Jasmine blurted. "I was getting hot." She glanced at her friends to see if they were accepting her explanations and saw that all three of them were still squinting at her. She was a horrible liar, always stammering or talking way too fast. They all probably knew that her alterations had nothing to do with a soap spill. Thankfully, none of them called her on it.

"Well, if you're all set, we should go," Theresa said. "I need to neaten up my locker before homeroom."

Something about Theresa's statement sounded all too familiar. Jasmine shot a quick look at Carrie and Anna, and all three of them giggled.

"Hey—a messy locker is a sign of genius," Theresa told them with a scowl. But as they started down the hall, she, too, started to laugh. "All right, you might as well know, Jasmine. I'm still the queen of clutter."

"That's okay, Resa," Carrie said. "I'm still the queen of crazy hair."

"Are you kidding? I love your hair!" said Anna. "It's naturally curly."

Carrie held a strand of her hair out in front of her face and examined it. "It's naturally *something*," she said. "But I can't do anything with it."

"That's because you never try," Theresa said.

Carrie shrugged. "I guess," she said. "But that's because I don't like playing around with my hair. I'd rather just let it dry and stick a barrette in it."

Jasmine smiled. It had been two years, but it seemed that Carrie and Theresa hadn't changed that much after all. "I think your hair looks good like that," Jasmine said. "It's carefree and fun."

"Thanks," Carrie said. "Coming from the queen of fashion, that's a big compliment."

"The queen of fashion?" Jasmine repeated. Was Carrie making fun of her? Jasmine studied her friend's face. Carrie didn't look like she was being sarcastic, but how else could she possibly say such a thing after seeing what Jasmine was wearing that morning and how out of place she was? "I don't think so," Jasmine replied.

"Oh, yes you are," Theresa said. "You always had cool clothes, and you obviously still do. That zebra skirt is great . . . when it's turned right-side out. Where did you get it, anyway?"

Jasmine winced. She knew her friends were trying to make her feel better after Ashley's assault, but she wished they'd stop drawing attention to her clothes. She was trying to fit in, not stand out. "I made it last night," she muttered, hoping that now they could leave the subject of her clothing alone for a while.

No such luck. The mouths of the three other girls dropped open. "You *made* it?" Carrie asked.

"Last night?" said Theresa.

"That's awesome!" Anna exclaimed. "I can't believe you can make your own clothes."

Jasmine grimaced. She wished they would keep their voices down. "Hey, what about Anna?" she asked, trying to shift the focus to someone else. "What's she the queen of?"

Theresa paused, but only for a moment. "Anna is the queen of quick comebacks."

"That's for sure," Carrie agreed.

Anna smiled. "I like that," she said. "I was afraid you were going to make me the queen of people under four feet five."

The other girls laughed, and Carrie said, "I swear, Anna—you should do stand-up for the talent show. You're so funny!"

Jasmine paused, glancing back at her friends

as they turned down a second hallway. "Talent show?" she asked. "What talent show?"

"Oh, that's right—you don't know about it," Carrie said.

"It's going to be awesome," Theresa gushed.

"The eighth grade is putting on a talent show as a fund-raiser. Anyone at Elizabeth Cady Stanton Middle School can be in it, and they're giving away prizes for the best acts," Anna said.

"Gift certificates to different stores, CDs, movie passes, cash—a bunch of cool stuff," Theresa added.

"Wow. That does sound like fun," Jasmine said. "We were supposed to have a talent show at my old school in Boston this spring, too. A few of my friends and I were talking about doing something for it, but I had to move before we could get anything together."

"That's too bad," Carrie said. "Maybe you can do something for this one instead."

"Are any of you doing anything?" Jasmine asked.

Anna shook her head. "Not me. After helping with the fifth-grade play and the Spring Carnival, I'm looking forward to just sitting back and watching for once."

"Me, too," Theresa said. "What about you, Carrie?"

"I think I might sing something," Carrie said, "if I can come up with a good song."

"That's great, Carrie," Jasmine said. "I wish I could sing. It would be fun to do something for the talent show, but I don't think I have a talent."

Carrie clicked her tongue. "Of course you have a talent," she said. "Everybody's good at something."

"Yeah," Theresa said. "Like juggling. Can you juggle?"

Jasmine shook her head. "No."

"What about dancing?" Anna suggested. "Ballet? Jazz? Tap?"

"No, no, and no," Jasmine replied.

"How about . . . acting something out?" Carrie said. "You know, like reciting a poem or doing a scene from a play?"

Jasmine frowned. "I'm not sure I'd be good at that, either."

"Even if you were, it wouldn't matter," said a voice right behind her. "I'm doing a song from *My Fair Lady,* and I plan to win the prize for Most Talented Overall."

Jasmine stiffened. It had been nearly two years, but she could still recognize that voice—and that attitude—anywhere.

"Sharon Ross," she said, whirling around.

"Jasmine Porter," Sharon replied, darting a look at Jasmine's feet. "Nice boots."

Jasmine felt her skin growing hot again and wished she could fade into the background.

"Hello? I said nice boots," Sharon repeated.

Jasmine narrowed her eyes and examined Sharon's face. She seemed sincere. "Oh," Jasmine said, "I thought you were . . ." Her voice trailed off.

"What?" Sharon asked.

Jasmine shook her head. "Nothing. Thanks," she said, feeling more confused than ever. This place was going to take some getting used to.

CHAPTER Two

In homeroom, things went a little bit more smoothly for Jasmine. Mrs. Wessex, Jasmine's new homeroom, English, and social studies teacher, had been really nice. She'd introduced Jasmine to the class and made her feel welcome without making a big deal about the fact that she was new, which almost made up for the fact that the two girls who sat in the front corner, Lauren Graham and Maria Mancini, kept glancing at Jasmine and smirking at her the same way Ashley had earlier that morning. Jasmine had done her best to ignore them, and it helped when Carrie, Theresa, and Anna introduced her to some more new friends—three boys who seemed pretty cool.

Jasmine had attended first through third grade with two of them—Matt Dana and Kevin Hathaway—but she'd never been in the same homeroom as them. The third boy, Spence, was new this year. He'd transferred to ECS just a few weeks after Anna, although Jasmine never would have guessed that he'd only been there for a month and a half. Just like Anna, he seemed to have fit right in. And now, as she sat in art class, Jasmine was hoping she could do the same. It was never fun to be the new kid. She was hoping she wouldn't have to wear the label for very long.

"Yo—nice work, Jazzy P.," a voice called from behind her. Jasmine jumped slightly. She'd been focused on gluing a triangle of fabric onto a piece of Bristol board, and Spence's comment had surprised her.

"Thanks," she said.

"Hey—that *is* cool, Jasmine," Theresa said from the next stool over. She, Carrie, Anna, and Jasmine were sharing a table, and Spence, Kevin, Matt, and Jeremy Gray were sitting at the one just behind them.

"Let me see," Anna said as she and Carrie leaned across the table.

"Cool," Carrie commented. "I wish I had artistic talent."

"Maybe you do," Jasmine replied. *You just need an idea and a plan,* she thought. It was a phrase her art teacher in Boston, Ms. Dennick, had always used—a phrase that had helped Jasmine grow to love art class. And now it was a phrase that made her miss Boston. Although Ms. Hamlin, the art teacher at ECS, seemed pretty cool, too.

She'd started the class by giving every student a piece of bristol board and every table a clear plastic bin full of fabric scraps, beads, and yarn. Then she'd instructed the students to work on making collages. It was the kind of free-form project that Jasmine loved. They could cut the fabric into any shapes they wanted and apply the materials to the board in any pattern at all. They were starting with nothing and they could finish with anything—a possibility that always excited Jasmine.

Jasmine had opted to first use a felt-tip pen to create several stick figures in different poses. Then she had cut her fabric scraps to create outfits for each of them. And now she was looking down at a board that was half-covered with her original clothing designs.

"I like *that* one," Theresa said, pointing to a figure near the middle of the board. The one she'd singled out was sporting a sleeveless aqua tee with a ruffled front—which Jasmine had created by layering thin lengths of fabric side by side—plaid capri pants with flared bottoms, and a tan hat with a narrow brim and a daisy poking out of it.

"That's totally you, Resa," Carrie said.

"Yeah," Anna agreed. "You'd look awesome in that. Too bad it's not your size."

Theresa's eyes lit up. "I bet Jasmine could make it my size," she said with a grin. "She made her skirt."

"That's true," Carrie said.

"Could you, Jasmine?" Theresa asked.

Jasmine squinted at the outfit in question. "Yeah, I guess. The pants would be pretty easy, and I guess I could do the shirt, too, if I had the fabric."

"Really?" Theresa said, her dark brown eyes sparkling. "I mean, could you *really* make that outfit for me?"

Jasmine shrugged. "I think so. I could probably even make that hat if I had some felt and a nice ribbon."

"That is *so* cool, Jasmine," Carrie said. "You're like . . . a fashion designer."

"She's a fashion designer / a real Calvin Kleiner / and like a diamond to the miner / nothin' could be finer," Spence rapped from the next table.

Jasmine blinked rapidly, staring at Spence. "Was that just off the top of your head?" she asked.

"It was off the top of somewhere," Spence said. "All the stuff I said just comes outta my head. I'll be bringing it till I'm dead," he added, much to Jasmine's amazement. She clapped and grinned.

"Now, *that's* a talent," she said.

"And he's just getting warmed up," Carrie replied. "You should hear him when he really lets loose."

"I'll bet," Jasmine said. Then she turned to Spence. "So, are you rapping for the talent show?"

"I've been thinking about it," he said.

"You should, Spence. It'd be *so* cool to hear you do a whole song," Carrie said.

"Yeah, and Kevin could beat-box for you," Anna suggested.

"Someone talking about me?" Kevin asked, turning around on his stool.

"We were just saying that you and Spence should do a rap for the talent show," Theresa explained. "You on the beat box and Spence on the mike."

At the mention of beat boxing, Kevin brought his hands to his mouth and rattled off a series of percussive beats that made it sound like he had a whole drum kit playing.

"Oh, no, here they go," Matt said, smirking.

"Matty D. says, 'Oh, no / here they go with the talent show,' / we can kick it fast or slow / we can go all day, you know / bringin' beats and slingin' rhymes / keepin' fresh in double time / you like lemon, I got lime / but it all goes down just fine—"

"Ahem."

As quickly as Kev and Spence had started up, they stopped. "Yo, Ms. Hamlin—what's shakin'?" Spence asked.

"How's your work coming along, gentlemen?" the art teacher asked. Jasmine, Carrie, Anna, and Theresa were all biting their tongues, trying not to burst out laughing.

"Pretty good," Kevin, Matt, and Jeremy all replied as Jasmine snuck a look at their boards. Kevin was using his fabric to create a woodland scene, complete with a stream and a couple of deer, and Matt was in the process of gluing on a small circle of charcoal-colored felt that was one of the wheels on his elaborately designed skateboard. She couldn't quite see what Jeremy's was, but it looked like a stained glass window, and he appeared to be about halfway done. Spence, on the other hand, had plenty of glue on his fingers but only a few random scraps of fabric on his board.

"Masterpieces take time, Ms. H.," Spence told her.

"Yes, they do," Ms. Hamlin agreed. "And we don't have much left, so I suggest that you try to stay focused."

"Thanks, Ms. H.," Spence said with a grin. "Words to live by."

Ms. Hamlin pressed her lips together and narrowed her eyes, but then, in spite of the fact that Spence had been goofing off only two seconds earlier, she smiled at him and just shook her head. Then she moved on to the next table to check on other students' progress. As soon as she was gone, Jasmine gaped at her friends.

"Does he always get away with stuff like that?" she asked. All three girls nodded.

"Teachers *love* Spence," Theresa whispered.

Jasmine smiled. She could see why. He was so upbeat and funny—the kind of person nobody could stay angry at, no matter how hard they tried. Jasmine replayed part of his rhyme in her head and started to chuckle, but when she glanced toward the art room entryway, the smile faded from her face.

Through the small window in the wooden door, she could see Ashley Dutton pointing and laughing. *At her.* And even worse, Maria Mancini and Lauren Graham were looking from Ashley to Jasmine and back again, shaking with silent laughter.

Jasmine's heart sank. Amazing. Here she was, surrounded by friends, happy and laughing and having a good time. Yet with just one cruel look, Ashley Dutton and her cohorts had managed to make her feel completely alone.

CHAPTER Three

For the rest of the day, Jasmine managed to more or less ignore Maria and Lauren and pretty much avoid Ashley, who, as a sixth grader, had most of her classes in a separate wing. But at the end of the day, while Jasmine was waiting for her mother to pick her up, she'd had to endure one more encounter with them. The three girls—who Jasmine had come to realize were close friends despite being in different grades—had walked past her on their way to their bus, giggling as Ashley called out, "I can't wait to see what she shows up in tomorrow!" which brought more snickers from the rest of the line for the bus.

Being singled out and mocked so openly made Jasmine's stomach flip, and she knew she couldn't take another day of it. She stared at the pavement until she heard her mom's horn beep, then she climbed inside the car and looked at her mother.

"Mom, can we stop at that thrift shop we passed on our way in this morning?" she asked immediately.

"What for?" Mrs. Porter replied.

"I just want to check it out," Jasmine said. "It's new—it wasn't there two years ago and I want to see what they have."

"Well—"

"Besides, didn't you say you needed a new lamp for your bedroom? I'm pretty sure their sign said something about home furnishings," Jasmine added.

"Did it?" Mrs. Porter asked, and from the way she was furrowing her brow, Jasmine knew she almost had her.

"Mm-hm. I think I even saw a couple of floor lamps in the window."

Mrs. Porter raised her eyebrows. Jasmine knew her mother had wanted an adjustable swing-arm floor lamp to put next to her desk for a long time. "Hmm. I guess we could stop for a minute," Mrs. Porter said, and Jasmine smiled. Sometimes her mother was *so* easy to manipulate. "But Jasmine," she added with a sideways glance, "not too long with the clothes, okay? And I don't want to spend a lot of money. I'll get you a few new things for school, but let's not go overboard."

Jasmine smiled awkwardly. "Thanks, Mom," she said. Okay, so maybe it wasn't so much that her mother was easy to manipulate—maybe it was more that Jasmine was easy to read. Either way, it didn't matter. The important thing was that Jasmine was going to be able to pick up some plain old boring, bland clothes that would keep her from standing out.

As Jasmine stepped out of her mother's car the next morning, she felt confident that she'd accomplished her goal. She'd managed to score two pairs of blue jeans, three fairly plain T-shirts, and her current outfit: a long-sleeved white tee underneath a simple lavender linen tank dress. Totally un-mockable.

It felt kind of strange to be dressed in such ordinary clothes. In Boston, Jasmine had enjoyed mixing and matching trends to create her own styles, and it had definitely been fun to start designing and making her own clothes, but this wasn't Boston. It was Newcastle, New Hampshire, and more than anything, she wanted to fit in, even if it meant wearing boring things.

"Hey, Jasmine," Anna called, running up to

meet her. Jasmine glanced nervously around the courtyard, but no one else seemed to have noticed her arrival. *Phew. So far, so good,* she thought. As she and Anna walked over to join Carrie and Theresa, Jasmine kept darting looks to the left and right. As far as she could tell, no one was laughing at her today. At least for now.

"You look nice," Carrie said.

Jasmine glanced down at the pale purple dress and sighed. It was even more boring than she remembered. The only thing that made it remotely interesting was a small silver button on one of the pockets that was shaped like a princess. "Thanks," she said.

"Did you make that dress?" Theresa asked.

Jasmine almost laughed. If she'd designed the dress herself, she would have trimmed the length and made it a lot funkier, but her days of giving her clothes pizzazz were over. At least for now.

"No, I bought this one," she told her friends.

"I figured," Theresa said. "Your zebra skirt was so cool. And your dress is, too," she added quickly, "it's just that it's so . . . *normal.* I guess I was kind of hoping you'd be wearing another original outfit today."

"Oh," Jasmine said, "well, actually, I don't wear that zebra skirt or any of the other stuff I had on yesterday very often. It was just that . . . all my other clothes were dirty," she lied. "I don't even own any other funky clothes. In fact, I guess I'm really kind of a boring dresser when you get right down to it," she added with a nervous laugh.

Theresa glanced at her sideways and Jasmine knew she'd said too much. *I've really got to work on my lying,* she thought. She stared down at her plain tan sandals and bit her lip. If she stopped babbling for a minute, maybe her friends would just forget about her clothes and move on.

It was quiet for a moment, and when Jasmine looked up, she saw the three girls mouthing something to one another and exchanging cryptic looks. "What's going on?" she asked. But instead of explaining, the girls just smiled as Theresa unclasped a bracelet from her wrist, and handed it to Jasmine.

"What's this?" Jasmine asked, taking the silver chain in her hand.

"It's a charm bracelet," Theresa said.

"A very *special* charm bracelet," Carrie added. "It helped all of us when we really needed it—kind of brought us good luck, you know?"

"We each added one of the charms that are on there," Theresa said. "I put the fairy on."

"And I added the unicorn," Carrie said.

"The angel was mine," Anna put in.

Jasmine looked at each of the three girls in turn and then focused on the bracelet, examining each of the tiny silver figures. "This is really pretty, but I can't take this from you," she said, trying to hand the bracelet back to Theresa.

"It's not just from me," Theresa said, pushing the bracelet back toward Jasmine. "It's from all of us."

"Yeah," Anna said, "and you can't give it back to all three of us without breaking it."

"But—"

"Just think of it as a welcome-back gift," Carrie said.

Jasmine gazed at the three girls and knew that not keeping the bracelet wasn't an option. With a quick smile, she clasped the bracelet around her wrist and admired it for a moment. The silver chain was cool against her skin, and the charms sparkled in the sunlight. "Thanks, you guys," she said. "It's really nice."

"And it's lucky, too," Theresa reminded her.

Just then, a loud giggle erupted from Ashley Dutton, who was walking toward them. Jasmine fingered the silver chain. *I hope so,* she thought. *Because it looks like I'm going to need it.*

"Oh, my God! I can't believe it!" Ashley cried as

she crossed the courtyard. She was pointing straight at Jasmine and laughing her head off. Maria and Lauren were right next to her, as were a few of their sixth- and seventh-grade friends, but none of them seemed to have gotten the joke yet. They were smirking, but only tentatively, as if they weren't sure what was so funny. Jasmine was puzzled, too. She couldn't imagine what Ashley found so amusing about her plainer-than-plain clothes.

Carrie, Anna, and Theresa were all watching Ashley's approach. It would have been hard not to—she was making such a big scene.

"I can't believe it," Ashley said as she and her crew walked up to Jasmine's group. "Yesterday was bad enough, but now—" She burst into giggles, and the others joined in with hesitant laughter, still looking a bit confused.

"What?" Jasmine said. "What are you laughing at?"

"That dress." Ashley giggled.

Jasmine's heart was pounding and she wished Ashley would just leave her alone, but she was so curious that she couldn't help responding. "What's wrong with it?"

Ashley brought her hand to her face and wiped tears from her eyes. "It's mine!" she blurted. Jasmine stiffened, uncertain what

Ashley meant but knowing that it couldn't be good.

"What are you talking about?" Theresa demanded, hands on her hips.

"It's *my* dress," Ashley repeated. "I donated it to Goodwill last month!" Again Lauren, Maria, and all the others burst out laughing, and Jasmine felt her face flushing red. It couldn't be true, could it? She couldn't possibly have picked out a dress that used to belong to Ashley Dutton. Jasmine glanced at all of her friends, but none of them seemed to know quite what to say. Even Anna appeared to be at a loss.

"What's your problem, Ashley?" Sharon Ross demanded, stepping off the basketball court with a ball tucked under one arm. "It's a plain purple dress. Even if you did give one like that to Goodwill, that doesn't mean Jasmine's wearing it. You can get a boring dress like that anywhere."

Jasmine swallowed hard. She was glad that Sharon had stepped in to defend her, but she wished that the words *plain* and *boring* hadn't been used in her defense.

"Not one with a princess on it," Ashley said with a smug smile.

"What are you—?" Jasmine started, but then

it hit her. The silver button. Ashley was referring to the silver princess button sewn onto the pocket.

"What are you talking about, Dutton?" Sharon demanded.

"That button," Ashley said, pointing at the pocket of Jasmine's dress. "It's shaped like a princess. My mother thought it was cute, so she sewed it on in place of the regular button, but I thought it was babyish, and I never wore the dress again. Then finally, last month, I stuck it in a bag to go to Goodwill."

Jasmine shuddered. It was true. She was wearing one of Ashley Dutton's castoffs.

"You know, Jasmine, I have another bag of old, outdated clothes almost ready to go. Should I just bring them to your house this time and save you a trip?" Ashley's minions positively cackled, and it seemed to Jasmine that some of the other students in the courtyard had joined in, too.

Tears began to form in Jasmine's eyes, but there was no way she could handle the additional humiliation of letting Ashley see her cry. She picked up her book bag and headed for the school, increasing her speed with every step.

"Jasmine!" she heard someone call, but she didn't want to know who it was. It could have been one of her friends, but it could also have been one of Ashley's lackeys with another cruel remark. So instead of turning around, Jasmine walked straight into the school, down the hall, and into the girls' bathroom, where she promptly ripped the princess button off her dress and threw it into the metal trash can.

She heard it clang once as it hit the side and again as it hit bottom. Then she kicked the trash can for good measure, brought her hands to her face, and began to sob.

"Oh, gross!" someone exclaimed, causing Jasmine to jump. She glanced around, but the bathroom appeared to be empty. Bending over, she checked under all the stall doors for feet but saw no one. Then she heard the voice again.

"Would you please get me out of here? This is disgusting!"

Jasmine narrowed her eyes and looked around. There was no one else in sight, yet the voice was loud and clear. And it seemed to be coming from the garbage can.

Slowly, Jasmine leaned forward and peered over the edge. Tissues, paper towels, a broken pencil—nothing unusual—until the contents of the trash can started to rustle, as though something were moving underneath it all! In a few seconds, to Jasmine's amazement, a small hand appeared and then another, as a tiny figure hoisted itself up onto one of the paper towels. Jasmine's jaw dropped, and she watched as the little creature dusted itself off and gazed up at her.

"I gotta say," the small being announced, cocking her head, "that is *no* way to treat a princess."

CHAPTER Four

"I—I—I—" Jasmine stammered. She had to be imagining this. "I . . ."

"I know. You're sorry," the little figure said. Then she shrugged. "Fuhgetaboutit," she added, slurring the sentence into one long word.

"Um . . . *okay,*" Jasmine said.

"But you know, there is somethin' you could do to make it up to me," the tiny person went on. Jasmine just stared. The little figure cupped her hands around her mouth. "Hello? Are you gettin' this?" she yelled.

"Oh . . . yeah," Jasmine replied.

"Well, then, ya think you could get me outta here?"

"Right—sorry," Jasmine said. She bent down and held out her hand tentatively, half expecting to wake up and find that she was still in bed and that this whole morning had been a dream. But instead the little creature climbed onto Jasmine's palm, her weight and the tickling sensation of her high-heeled shoes proving that she was, in fact, real.

"Phew! Thanks," she said, straightening out her long yellow dress and adjusting the diminutive diamond crown on her head. "I mean, a trash can's no place for a princess, am I right?"

"Ummm . . ." Jasmine muttered, staring at the tiny girl in her hand.

"'Cause princesses can't stand trash and dirt and grime and grease and stuff, right?"

"Uh . . . I guess." Jasmine nodded.

"And since *I* am a princess—which you probably already guessed on account of my lovely gown and my jewels and my tiara and my beautifully groomed, long blond locks—it makes sense that I'd be squeamish about all that stuff, too, right?"

"Yeah," Jasmine said. "Sure."

"You do believe I'm a princess, don'tcha?" the tiny sprite asked, leaning forward.

"I'm not sure what to believe," Jasmine said. Then she remembered the button. "Wait a minute," she said. She set the princess on top of the metallic soap dispenser and peered down into the trash. She moved a few paper towels aside so that she could see to the bottom of the can, but there was no sign of the silver princess button she'd torn from her dress.

"You're not gonna find it," the princess said. "It's not in there."

"How do you know?" Jasmine asked.

"Because *I'm* out here."

"You mean—?"

"Mm-hm." The little figure nodded.

"But . . . how?"

"Bada boom, bada bing," the princess replied with a snap of her fingers. "That's the way we move between dimensions—we find a representation of ourselves and sort of . . . materialize through it."

"You . . . what?"

"Fuhgetaboutit," the princess said again. "It's not important. What's important is what's got you so riled up at the moment. What's goin' on?"

Jasmine groaned, remembering why she had thrown the button in the trash in the first place, never mind how crazy it was that her button had just come alive. "This isn't *my* dress," she said.

"Whadd'ya mean?"

"The dress I'm wearing. It used to belong to a girl named Ashley Dutton. But she gave it to Goodwill and I bought it."

"Ohhh. So it's your dress now, but it's still kinda like you're wearin' someone else's dress, huh?"

"Yeah, especially since Ashley made a point of telling everyone in the courtyard about it." Jasmine ran her hands through her hair and shook her head. What was she going to do now? Turning her clothes inside out wasn't an option this time around.

"Psst!" hissed the little princess, leaning forward. Jasmine looked down at her. "Can ya keep a secret?"

Jasmine squinted. What was this about? "I guess," she said.

The princess's eyes darted left and then right, and then she leaned even farther forward and cupped one hand beside her mouth. "I'm wearin' somebody else's dress, too," she whispered.

"Huh?"

The princess cupped her hands in front of her mouth again. "I said, 'I'm wearin' somebody else's—' "

"I heard what you said," Jasmine interrupted. "I'm just not sure why you're saying it. Are you trying to tell me that where you come from, princesses shop at Goodwill, too?"

The little princess shook her head and

grinned. "That's the thing," she said with a mischievous giggle. "I'm not really a princess."

Jasmine eyed the tiny figure up and down. "You certainly look like one," she said.

"Thanks," the not-princess replied. "We were hopin' I could pull it off, but I'm tellin' you—it hasn't been easy. Of course, it doesn't matter so much if *you* know the truth, but if the queen found out, whew! The two of us would be in it up to our tiaras."

"*What* are you talking about?" Jasmine asked.

"Oh, sorry. I guess I should explain," said the little person, removing her crown. She rubbed the top of her head and grimaced. "Man, that thing makes my head itch." She scratched her scalp a few times, mussing up her honey-blond hair, then gave a sigh of relief and looked up at Jasmine.

"The name's Ruby, by the way," she said, extending her tiny hand, which Jasmine shook with her thumb and forefinger. "And I'm actually an auto mechanic. You know, a regular, old grease monkey. But the thing is, the princess, Sarah, is a good friend of mine, and it just so happens that we look a lot alike."

"So you switched places?" Jasmine asked.

"Yeah—just for a couple of weeks, though.

See, Sarah needed a break from all of her 'royal duties.' She said it gets real tirin' always havin' to make public appearances and look nice and be nice and pose for pictures and stuff, so she asked me to take over for a while so she could get a little R & R—you know, rest and relaxation—like a normal person."

Jasmine smiled. "Hey, that's kind of like that story 'The Prince and the Pauper,' you know?"

"Yeah, except that she's not a prince and I'm no pauper. Auto mechanics make pretty decent money, ya know. Especially if they're good—and I am. I can find and fix any problem faster and better than anyone else in town, so I figure I should probably be able to handle this assignment, too."

"What assignment?" Jasmine asked.

"What assignment," Ruby echoed, laughing and slapping her knee. "You're a hoot."

"No, really—what assignment?" Jasmine asked.

Ruby squinted. "You mean you don't know?"

"Know what?"

"Aw, shoot—I thought that was how this was supposed to work."

"How what was supposed to work?" Jasmine asked.

"This whole thing," Ruby said. "Me comin' here to help you."

"You came here to help me?"

"Yeah," Ruby replied, scratching her head again. "At least, I think so. See, one of the princess's duties is to act as a sort of goodwill ambassador to the seventh dimension, which is here, where you live. And what she does is kinda travel around helpin' people solve their problems. So when I got paged to come here, I figured that you'd have a problem for me to help you with. You do, don'tcha?"

Jasmine thought for a moment. "Not really. I mean, there's Ashley Dutton, but she's a person, not a problem."

"Believe me—people can be problems. You'd know that if you knew the queen," Ruby said. "This Ashley Dutton—she's the one who gave away the dress, right?"

"That's her," Jasmine said.

"And what else has she done?" Ruby asked. "I mean, is it just the thing with the dress, or is there other stuff?"

"Oh, there's other stuff," Jasmine said. "There's always been other stuff with Ashley. She just doesn't like me, so she picks on me and makes fun of me every chance she gets. She started back in third grade, when some guy she liked decided he liked me instead, and she's been doing it ever since. Well—actually, I moved away for a couple of years, but now that I've moved back, she's started right back in on me. And this time it's not just Ashley. Everyone here seems to think I'm weird. And no matter how hard I try, I can't seem to fit in."

"Hmmm," Ruby said, tapping her finger against her lips. "Sounds like a problem to me. That must be what I'm here to help you with."

"I guess," Jasmine said. "But just how are you supposed to help me?"

Ruby shrugged. "I'm not sure. There was a NASCAR race on TV when Sarah was explainin' all that stuff, so I kinda missed a lot of the details," she admitted. "I do know, however, that this tiara," she said, holding up the diamond-encrusted crown, "is supposed to be enchanted."

"Enchanted?"

"Yeah, sort of like a magic wand, ya know? So maybe I can use it to help you. If I can figure out how it works."

"You don't know how it works?" Jasmine asked. Somehow she doubted that this little mechanic was going to be much help.

"I told you—*NASCAR*. But I'll figure it out," Ruby said, turning the tiara over in her hands. "After all, it can't be more complicated than rebuildin' an engine. Can it?"

CHAPTER
Five

Sign Up Today for the
Fifth Annual 8th-Grade Talent Show!
Prizes for
Best in Grade, Most Talented Overall,
Most Unique Talent, Best Solo Performer, and More!
Tickets on sale at the school store.
All proceeds to benefit the 8th-Grade River
Steward program and end-of-year class trip.

"What's the River Steward program?" Jasmine asked as she and Anna read the flyer on Mrs. Wessex's door.

"It's some kind of project the eighth graders have been working on. I think they're responsible for helping to keep a section of a river clean or something like that," Anna said. "And then at the end of the year they get to go camping and ride a raft through the part they helped take care of. It sounds pretty cool."

"I hope we get to do something like that when we're in eighth grade."

"Yeah," Anna said. Then she gasped. "Oh, no—Jasmine, look!" she exclaimed. Jasmine glanced around, worried that Anna had spotted Ashley Dutton nearby, even though there was nothing about Jasmine's clothes that Ashley could criticize today. Jasmine had made sure of it this time.

She was wearing the blue jeans she'd bought at the thrift shop and a plain pink T-shirt, and before putting either of them on, she'd searched them both thoroughly to make sure there weren't any distinguishing details that indicated they might once have belonged to Ashley Dutton. Her outfit was beyond boring this time, and Jasmine had kept it that way despite Ruby's insistence that it didn't suit her and that she should spice it up a little.

Still, the urgent tone of Anna's voice worried her. Jasmine gazed up and down the hallway, left and right and all around, but the coast seemed to be clear. "What?" she asked Anna finally. "I don't see anything."

"No—not in the hall," Anna said. She tapped the sheet of notebook paper that was taped to the wall below the flyer. "Up here. Today is the last day to sign up to be in the talent show."

Jasmine read the sentence Anna was pointing to and shrugged. "So?" she asked. "I didn't think you were planning to do anything."

"I'm not," Anna said, "but I thought you wanted to."

"Yeah, I did," Jasmine said with a sigh. "But I never came up with an idea."

"Ooh—this sounds like another problem," Ruby said, popping out of the front pocket of Jasmine's book bag. "Maybe I'm supposed to help you out with the talent show. Do ya think that could be why I'm here?"

Jasmine glanced down at the little auto-mechanic-turned-princess and shrugged. She knew Anna couldn't see Ruby. Before they had left the girls' bathroom yesterday, Ruby had explained that she was only visible to the person she was there to help, and that she had to be kept a secret—that was one of the few details she'd managed to catch during the NASCAR race. But people could, of course, hear Jasmine, and if they did, they'd think she was talking to herself. So Jasmine had to communicate with Ruby via signals and facial expressions whenever they were with other people.

"I could teach you to do an oil change in less than five minutes," Ruby offered. "Or maybe you could rotate someone's tires onstage. Could we get a car up there?"

Jasmine lowered one eyebrow and gazed down at her little friend.

"Yeah, I guess that would be a little too sophisticated," Ruby said. "People wouldn't be able to appreciate the technical expertise involved. If I could just figure out how this tiara works," she said, fidgeting with one of the diamonds, "then maybe I could help you out." She grasped the ends of the tiara in both hands, held it at arm's length, and shouted, "Hocus-pocus!"

Jasmine gaped as a spark shot out of the uppermost part of the tiara and grazed the shoulder of an older boy who just happened to be passing by. Suddenly the boy stopped walking, dropped to the ground, and did an amazing break-dance move that began with a handstand and ended with a super-fast back spin.

Everyone who had seen his impromptu performance burst into applause and cheered for him, but when the boy finally stopped spinning, he looked confused—as if he wasn't sure how he had gotten onto the floor or what he was doing there. Slowly he got up and dusted himself off, squinting suspiciously at everyone in the hallway, as though they had all conspired to play a cruel trick on him. Many of the students were still applauding for him, but he didn't seem to notice. Instead he backed away cautiously, turning and practically sprinting once he'd reached a safe distance.

"That was weird," Anna said, staring after him.

That was Ruby, Jasmine thought, and she glared down at the little mechanic.

"Whoa, baby! I guess there's some talent in this tiara after all!" Ruby whooped. "I admit, that wasn't quite what I was goin' for, but it's a start."

Jasmine continued to glare.

"Tell you what—I'll just be in here if you need me," Ruby said, and she dived—tiara and all—back down into Jasmine's book bag pocket.

Once she was safely inside, Jasmine turned back to the sign-up sheet—just in time to see Anna finish writing *Jasmine Porter* at the bottom of the list. "Anna!" she exclaimed. "What are you doing?"

"I'm signing you up," Anna said matter-of-factly.

"But I don't have a talent," Jasmine protested.

"Yes, you do," Anna said, and in the talent

column next to Jasmine's name she wrote *fashion.*

"Fashion isn't a talent," Jasmine said.

"You design and make your own clothes," Anna replied. "That's definitely a talent."

"But I don't," Jasmine lied. "I told you—that zebra skirt is practically the only thing I've ever made. I'm not even all that into fashion."

Anna cocked her head and gazed at Jasmine. Then she reached into Jasmine's book bag and plucked out the latest issue of *The Cutting Edge,* a fashion magazine for teens.

"That's—my mom's," Jasmine stammered. "I don't know how it got in there."

Anna pressed her lips together and frowned. "Come on, Jasmine, I know it's yours. And I know you like designing things. I've seen you sketching in math class. And that collage you started in art class was awesome."

Jasmine exhaled heavily, her shoulders slumping forward. "Look, even if I was into fashion, what would I do for an act?" she asked. "Bring in my mother's sewing machine and make everyone watch me stitch something together?"

"No," Anna said.

"Well, what, then?" Jasmine asked.

"You could take the sewin' machine apart

and put it back together!" Ruby's muffled voice called from inside the pocket. Jasmine ignored her.

"I don't know," Anna admitted. "But we don't need to know that yet. Right now we just need to get you signed up so you don't miss the deadline."

Jasmine took the pencil from Anna's hand and started to erase her name. "Anna, I don't think—"

"Oh, come on, Jasmine," Anna said, catching her friend's arm before she was able to take her name off the list. "If you don't sign up today, you won't be able to at all. And I'm sure you can come up with an act before the actual show. I'll help you. We all will—Carrie and Theresa, too."

"Well . . ." Jasmine said.

"How about this: you just leave your name up there for now. You know, just in case you decide you *do* want to do it. And if we don't come up with something good by the end of the week, you can drop out."

Jasmine thought it over. She had wanted to be in the talent show back in Boston, and it did sound like fun. "Um . . . okay," she said finally.

"Awesome!" Anna said, smiling. "I know we're going to come up with something really cool for you to do. And maybe you'll even win a prize. I heard the eighth graders have come up with a ton of categories, and I think one of the gift certificate prizes is from the local craft store. Wouldn't it be cool if you won that? Then you could buy more fabric and design some new clothes."

Jasmine's eyes lit up. There was nothing she enjoyed more than picking out really funky fabric and transforming it into a cool shirt or pants or a dress. Of course, now that she was living back in Newcastle, where blending in was the name of the game, she probably wouldn't be wearing a lot of her original designs. Unless, of course, she started designing boring clothes, but she didn't think she could bring herself to do that. It wouldn't be any fun.

Jasmine sighed. Looking just like everybody else wasn't exactly her preferred style. But unfortunately, it seemed to be her only option.

CHAPTER Six

"How did you guys do on that grammar test?" Carrie asked as she set her lunch bag on their usual table in the cafeteria.

"Okay," Theresa said, "but I'm pretty sure I messed up the sentence we had to diagram. I just don't get that stuff."

"Me, neither," Jasmine agreed. "I mean, I can get the subject and the verb in the right spots, but direct and indirect objects always mess me up. How about you, Anna?"

"I think I did all right," Anna said with a half shrug.

Theresa snorted. *"All right?"* she said. Then she turned to Jasmine. "Don't let her fool you, Jazzy. Anna isn't just the queen of putting people in their places. She's also the queen of acing tests. She always gets A's."

"Not always," Anna said.

"Oh, really? Have you done worse than an A on anything you've done since you moved here?" Theresa asked.

"Well . . . no," Anna admitted, "but—"

"Wow, Jasmine, I have to say, you have guts," Ashley Dutton interrupted, suddenly appearing at the end of the fifth graders' table.

Jasmine looked up and rolled her eyes. *Oh, great. Here we go again,* she thought. What could Ashley possibly be on about now?

"What do you mean?" Theresa asked.

"Your little friend here signed up for the talent show and listed her talent as . . ." Ashley paused to giggle, *"fashion!"*

Jasmine rubbed her forehead with one hand. She never should have let Anna put her name up there. It seemed like everything she did provided Ashley with more ammunition.

"Cool," Sharon said, adding her tray to the table. "So many people are just singing or doing some kind of dance routine—it'll be nice to have something different going on up there. Maybe you'll even win something, Jasmine."

Jasmine's eyes widened. This was the second time Sharon had jumped to her defense against Ashley.

"I think you missed the point, Sharon," Ashley said, scowling.

"I think you missed your table," Sharon replied. "Why don't you go sit down?"

"Ha! I like this Sharon girl. She's got spunk!" Ruby said. Jasmine, startled, glanced down at her lunch tray to see Ruby sitting on the edge, swinging her legs back and forth. She'd thought she left Ruby in her book bag in her locker, but apparently Ruby had found some way to tag along for lunch.

There was silence as Ashley and Sharon exchanged stony glares. Then Ashley's face softened and she looked back at Jasmine. "Anyway," she said, "before I was so rudely interrupted, I was going to ask you which of your clothing lines you're planning to feature in the talent show—your mismatched bag lady look, or last year's fashions, as purchased at Goodwill?"

"Ooh, she's nasty!" Ruby exclaimed.

"What's your problem, Ashley?" Theresa said. "Why don't you just leave Jasmine alone?"

"I'm not bothering her," Ashley said. "I'm just asking her about her amazing talent for fashion. I meant to say, Jasmine, today's outfit is your best yet. Jeans and a T-shirt—how bold."

"All right. That's enough outta her!" Ruby said. The tiny mechanic jumped up and stood on the rim of Jasmine's milk container, wielding the enchanted tiara and muttering strange syllables.

"Abracadabra, mchocus, salabra!" she shouted, and again Jasmine saw a bright spark shoot out of the tiara. It grazed the top of Ashley's perfect ponytail and landed on Kimberly Price's tray as she was coming to join Sharon and the others for lunch.

"Ouch!" Kimberly yelled when the spark made contact, and she jumped so high that her lunch tray flew out of her hands. Jasmine watched as chicken nuggets, fries, ketchup, applesauce, and milk rocketed into the air and landed—*BAM!*—on the floor, on the table, and on Theresa and Carrie, who were sitting at the end.

"Gross!" Theresa cried, staring at her outstretched palms as applesauce dripped off her fingers.

Carrie brushed a strand of milk-drenched hair away from her face. "Yuck," she groaned.

Remarkably, Ashley had remained untouched. "Whoa," she exclaimed, chuckling. "You know, Jasmine, maybe Kimberly can help you come up with some new fashions. She can just spatter food on some clothes and you can call it *cafeteria chic.*"

"I'm really sorry, guys," Kimberly said, using her napkin to try to wipe some of the food off Carrie and Theresa. "I don't know what happened. It was like my tray gave me a shock or something."

"Well, I'll let you girls get cleaned up," Ashley said. "Oh—and I can't wait to see your act, Jasmine," she added with a smirk before turning and walking back to her own table. Jasmine sighed and stared down at Ruby.

"This good-for-nothin' tiara!" Ruby shouted. "I think it needs a tune-up."

Jasmine just shook her head. Ruby's little stunt might have gotten Jasmine's friends covered in food, but at least it had gotten Ashley to leave her alone. For now. Jasmine wished more than anything that she could find some way to put Ashley in her place, but it would be nearly impossible for her to stand up for herself without standing *out,* and that was something she wasn't willing to risk.

CHAPTER Seven

"Okay, everyone," Ms. Hamlin called out at the beginning of art class. "Today is your last day to work on your fabric collages, so I want you all to get right to work and try to finish up."

"That's a tall order, Ms. Hamlin," Spence said as she handed him his barely begun piece.

"All the more reason for you to get right to it," the art teacher replied.

"Yo, no messin' around / artistic inspiration, I've suddenly found," Spence rhymed to Jasmine's table. Then he jumped onto his stool and began furiously gluing on the scraps of fabric he'd spent Monday cutting out.

Carrie giggled. "What did we do for entertainment before Spence transferred here?" she asked, and the others laughed, too.

"Oh, and if anyone needs a pencil sharpened," Ms. Hamlin added, "you'll have to use the manual one on the back wall. The electric one on my desk is jammed."

"Jammed?" Ruby said, hopping out of Jasmine's book bag and onto the table. "Did I hear someone say somethin's jammed?"

"The pencil sharpener," Jasmine murmured, leaning close to the table and pretending to cough.

"Oh, yeah! Let me at it! I can fix it!" Ruby pleaded, jumping up and down. Jasmine tilted her head and eyed the little mechanic. "I can," Ruby insisted. "Just walk by and plop me down next to it, and then pick me up again in fifteen minutes or so."

Jasmine shrugged. "Why not?" she muttered.

"What did you say?" Theresa asked.

"Nothing," Jasmine replied. "I just need to sharpen my pencil." She grabbed a pencil that looked reasonably dull, scooped Ruby up in her hand, and slid off her stool.

"Oh, baby!" Ruby said as Jasmine set her down on Ms. Hamlin's desk. "A real mechanical emergency—this is gonna be great! I'll have it working again in a flash." And with that, she scurried inside the sharpener, armed with a paper clip and a thumbtack, and set to work.

When Jasmine returned to her table, she saw

that Ms. Hamlin had finished passing out the rest of the collages.

"You're lucky, Jasmine," Theresa said, gesturing toward Jasmine's board. "You're almost done."

Jasmine examined her work. "Not really," she said. "I mean, I almost have all of the clothes done, but once I finish those, I want to use the beads and yarn to add jewelry and accessories."

"Wow," Anna said. "Your collage is going to be like a mini fashion-show."

"Totally," Theresa agreed. Then her eyes lit up. "Hey! You know what would be really cool?"

"What?" Jasmine asked.

"If you actually bought fabric and turned all of those designs into real clothes. You know, like we were saying the other day when I asked you if you could make those capri pants and that tank in my size."

"Yeah," Carrie said. "That *would* be cool. It would be like having your own clothing line."

"That's it!" Anna exclaimed.

Jasmine furrowed her brow. "That's what?"

"That's what you can do for the talent show!"

"What—show my collage to everybody?" Jasmine asked.

"No—do a fashion show!" Anna said.

"Who's doing a fashion show?" Sharon asked, stopping on her way back from the pencil sharpener.

"No one," Jasmine said.

"Oh, come on, Jasmine," Anna pleaded. "It would be so perfect. You could turn some of these designs into real clothes and then have people model them."

"And you could explain all of the outfits as people walked across the stage, just like they do in all those shows on the Fashion Channel," Theresa said.

"I don't think so, you guys," Jasmine said. Ever since Ashley's latest assault at lunch, Jasmine had been planning to drop out of the talent show. After all, the only reason Ashley had bothered her today was because she'd *signed up* for the talent show. If she could drop out and lay low for a while, maybe Ashley would forget about her altogether.

"Could you really make clothes like this?" Sharon asked, pointing at Jasmine's fabric collage.

Jasmine glanced down at the board and all of her quirky combinations. Everything she'd come up with was within her sewing ability—she'd just need to get the materials. "Well, *yes,* but—"

"Then you have to do it," Sharon said bluntly.

"I *have* to do it?" Jasmine asked.

"Mm-hmm." Sharon nodded. "You have to."

Jasmine screwed up her face. "Why?"

"Well, for one, these are cool designs and if you can really make all those clothes, you might actually have a shot at winning," Sharon said. Once again, Jasmine was surprised by the change in Sharon. Flat-out compliments weren't her usual style. "But the real reason you should do it is to put Ashley Dutton in her place," Sharon added.

"Wow, Sharon. I didn't know you disliked Ashley so much," Carrie said.

"I can't stand her," Sharon said. "She's so . . . bossy and snotty. And she thinks she knows everything. I can't stand people like that."

Jasmine glanced around the table and noticed that Carrie, Theresa, and Anna were all smirking ever so slightly, and Jasmine knew why. In some ways, Sharon and Ashley were very similar—not that any of them was about to point that out.

"I don't know, Sharon," Jasmine said. "I don't really think I'm up for it."

"Come on," Sharon prodded. "If you do a good job, you'll prove to her that you know a thing or two about fashion and she won't be able to tease you anymore."

"And if I do a bad job?" Jasmine asked.

Sharon shrugged. "Don't do a bad job and you won't have to worry," she said. Then she leaned closer to Jasmine. "Look, if you can really make these clothes, you should do it. The designs are cool, and a fashion show would be fun. I could model for you—I do have professional experience, you know."

Jasmine looked down at her collage and then back at Sharon and the rest of her friends. Maybe Sharon was right. Maybe doing a fashion show would prove to Ashley and the others that Jasmine wasn't the fashion victim they'd made her out to be. Maybe she could even get Ashley and company to back off while simultaneously encouraging a few other students to start wearing more interesting clothing.

Jasmine took a deep breath. "Okay," she said. "I'll do it."

Everyone at Jasmine's table, including Sharon, clapped and cheered, which, of course, brought Ms. Hamlin over to see what was going on. "Sharon, isn't your seat over there?" she asked, pointing to a table at the front of the room.

"On my way, Ms. Hamlin," Sharon said, skipping away before the teacher could say anything else to her.

"All right, ladies, we only have half an hour left. Let's try to be productive, shall we?"

"Yes, Ms. Hamlin," the girls chorused, and all of them began working again. Except for Jasmine. Grabbing another dull pencil from her bag, she headed for the pencil sharpener by way of Ms. Hamlin's desk.

"Ruby!" she whisper-hissed. "Are you—?"

"Finito!" Ruby exclaimed, climbing out of the front of the electric sharpener. "This baby's all set. Give 'er a try!"

Jasmine inserted her pencil into the front of the sharpener and listened to the soft whirring of its motor as it trimmed her lead to a perfect point. "Nice work," she said, admiring her pencil's ideally angled tip.

"Piece o' cake," Ruby said with a satisfied smile. "Got anything else that needs fixin'?"

"How about that dress?" Jasmine muttered.

Ruby's once pristine yellow gown was now tattered and torn all along the bottom, and the rest of it was covered with pencil lead, grease, and shavings. The tiny mechanic glanced down and gasped. "Rats! The princess is gonna toss me in the moat!" she cried. "What was I thinkin'? I can't wear fancy dresses—they just aren't me."

"I know what you mean," Jasmine said, catching a glimpse of her own outfit. She was sick of feeling so self-conscious all the time. Picking out clothes in the morning used to be one of her favorite parts of the day, but lately she'd been dreading it.

But if Sharon was right about the fashion show idea, and if Jasmine did a good job, maybe she'd be able to go back to wearing what she wanted again. It seemed like a long shot, but if it meant being able to be herself again, it was definitely worth a try.

CHAPTER Eight

"Mom," Jasmine blurted as soon as she opened the car door, "you need to take me to the fabric store right now, okay?"

"Oh, boy, big mistake!" Ruby said, slapping her forehead. "You can't just make a demand like that. You gotta work the angles first, prime the pump, you know?"

Jasmine scowled at the little mechanic, but then, as if to prove Ruby's point, Mrs. Porter frowned at her daughter. "I had a lovely day, thank you for asking, Jasmine. How was yours?"

"Ya see?" Ruby said, folding her arms across her chest and taking a seat on the passenger side headrest.

"Sorry," Jasmine said to her mother, buckling her seat belt. "I had a pretty good day, too," she said.

"I'm glad to hear it," Mrs. Porter said, pulling the car away from the curb.

"In fact," Jasmine went on, "I signed up for the school talent show—which is next week—and that's why I need you to take me to the fabric store. I'm going to do a fashion show and I only have until next Friday to make all of the clothes." By the time she was done speaking, Jasmine's voice had increased to whirlwind speed.

"Sheesh! Take a breath, why don'tcha?" Ruby admonished her.

And once again, Mrs. Porter seemed to agree with the little auto mechanic. "Slow down, Jasmine," her mother said. "Now, what's this about a talent show?"

"It's a fund-raiser for the eighth grade and I signed up to be in it. I'm going to design a bunch of clothes and do a mini fashion-show as my act." Even as the words came out of her mouth, Jasmine found herself surprised to hear them. She couldn't believe that she was actually going to do it—she was going to create and showcase her own original clothing line, and she was as nervous about it as she was excited.

"And you're planning to do all that in nine days?" Mrs. Porter said. "That's not a lot of time. Are you sure you can pull it off?"

"Of course she can!" Ruby cried out. "She's only got the finest mechanic in all nineteen dimensions on her side, right, Jazzy?"

Jasmine thought for a moment. She'd need at least eight outfits to be able to put on a decent fashion show, and that *would* be a lot of cutting and sewing. She'd have to complete a new outfit almost every day. "Well . . . no, I'm not sure," she admitted.

"What?" Ruby exclaimed. Jasmine put her index finger to her lips and frowned at Ruby. She needed a minute to think this through. The talent show was her chance to do her own fashion show *and* silence Ashley Dutton at the same time. The way Jasmine saw it, it was too great an opportunity to pass up.

"But I told my friends I was going to do it, and I want to at least try," she added. "So . . . do you think we could stop at the fabric store? I'll spend my own money. I still have a bunch saved from all the babysitting I did in Boston."

"Well," said Mrs. Porter. At the next stoplight, she glanced over at her daughter.

"Give 'er a smile," Ruby instructed. "And make it a good one." Jasmine did as she was told and gave her mother her most winning smile.

Mrs. Porter started to chuckle. "Oh, Jazzy," she said. "How can I say no to that? All right, we'll stop, but try to be quick. I'm probably just going to sit in the car and read."

"Thanks, Mom!" Jasmine gushed. "You're the best!" *And I'm going to show Ashley Dutton and everyone else at ECS that* I'm *the best when it comes to fashion*, she thought.

"I'm doomed!" Jasmine moaned, collapsing onto her bed.

"Come on, it can't be that bad," Ruby said. "Can it?"

Jasmine rolled onto her stomach and propped herself up on her elbows. "I don't see how it could be any worse," she said. "I couldn't find any decent fabric that I could afford more than a yard of, and every outfit that I want to make would take at least three—not to mention accessories. There's no way I'm going to be able to do a fashion show."

"Oh, quit whinin'," Ruby said. "You've got me here to help, remember?"

Jasmine squinted down at her tiny friend. So far, all she'd managed to do was make some boy break-dance in the hallway and cause Kimberly Price to bobble her lunch tray. Of course, Ruby *had* fixed the pencil sharpener, but that wasn't exactly the kind of skill that was going to help Jasmine put on a fashion show with no fashions.

"And I have this," Ruby added with a grin, holding up the tiara.

Jasmine winced. "I'm not sure that's such a good idea, Ruby," she said. "You haven't had much luck with it so far."

Ruby waved one tiny hand. "I was just workin' out the bugs before—third time's the charm," she assured Jasmine. "Now, what kinda fabric do you need?"

"Well," Jasmine started. "I saw some nice fleece that would be perfect for—"

Before Jasmine had even finished speaking, Ruby held the tiara up high in the air and cried, "Apples, peaches, pumpkin pie, give us fleece, and don't be shy!"

Thousands of tiny sparks flew out of the front of the tiara, and suddenly Jasmine's room filled with a strange fog that obscured everything.

"Ruby—what did you do?" Jasmine called, waving her arms in front of her face in an attempt to clear the air. After just a moment, it seemed to be working—the fog was thinning. When it cleared completely, Jasmine got the shock of her life.

"Ruby!" she yelled, staring wide-eyed at the creatures that now filled every square inch of her room. Ruby had conjured up a flock of sheep.

"Uh . . . oops," came Ruby's voice, although from where it was coming, Jasmine wasn't quite sure. The little mischief maker was nowhere to be seen.

"Oops?!" Jasmine yelled. "Is that all you have to say?"

"How 'bout 'baaa'?" Ruby replied. Jasmine grimaced and glanced around the room. She knew Ruby couldn't be too far away, but with all the sheep cluttering the space, it was hard to find a one-inch-tall auto mechanic.

"Just give me a second," Ruby called. "I'll fix it."

Finally, by following the sound of the tiny sprite's voice, Jasmine was able to locate her. Ruby was hopping across the sheeps' backs, heading for Jasmine's desk. When she got there, she held the tiara aloft once again and yelled, "I asked for fleece, but what I need is cotton, grown straight from the seed!" Once again the room was filled with blinding sparks and then a fog. Jasmine closed her eyes and listened.

"That's better," she heard Ruby say. *"Kind of."*

I don't want to know, Jasmine thought, but even so, she couldn't help opening her eyes to take a peek. This time, instead of twenty-something sheep, she was greeted by the sight of . . . cotton plants. "Ruby!" she exclaimed.

"Hey, it's better than a room full of livestock," Ruby argued.

"Not by much," Jasmine said. "What are we supposed to with all of this?"

Ruby shrugged. "Make fabric?"

"Of course!" Jasmine said, hitting her forehead with her hand exaggeratedly. "Why didn't I think of that? Just let me get out my spinning wheel and my loom. We should have plenty of fabric ready to go in . . . oh, *three months?*" She shook her head and rolled her eyes at the little mechanic.

"Is it that hard?" Ruby asked.

"Harder," Jasmine told her. Then she pressed her eyes closed and exhaled slowly. "I hate to ask this," she said finally, "but do you think you can get rid of it?"

"I'll give it a whirl," Ruby said. She took the tiara in two hands once again and held it up. Only this time, instead of calling out a confident incantation, she kind of winced and muttered. "Uh, cotton's cool and so is cash, but these plants have gotta go in the trash?"

Again there were sparks from the tiara, but this time there was no fog. Instead, the only things that appeared were a stack of biodegradable lawn and leaf bags and a bunch of twist ties at the end of Jasmine's bed.

"Great," Jasmine said. "This should only take an hour or so."

"Sorry," Ruby said with a frown. "I could try again," she offered, reaching for the tiara.

"No!" Jasmine cried. "Whatever you do, don't do any more magic with that thing!"

"Yeah," Ruby said, looking down at the diamond-encrusted crown. "I guess you're right. It really hasn't been much help."

"You can say that again," Jasmine replied as she began stuffing cotton plants into the plastic bags. "Not that it matters. It was stupid of me to think I could pull off a fashion show on such short notice anyway. I probably couldn't even do it if I had weeks to prepare. I'm just going to have to drop out and deal with Ashley making fun of me for that, too."

"Aw, don't say that, Jazzy," Ruby said. "We'll come up with—"

"Not now, Ruby," Jasmine whined. "I've got a lot of work to do." And she went back to packing up the cotton plants.

It did, indeed, take Jasmine about an hour to get all the cotton plants bagged and moved onto the front lawn for the recycling truck to pick up. Thankfully, her mother had gone to the grocery store, so Jasmine was able to take care of it all without her seeing. Then, as an added precaution, Jasmine placed the bags—all six of them—on the property line between her mom's house and the neighbor's house so that no one would really know who they belonged to.

"All right," Ruby said when Jasmine finally returned to her room. "Here's the plan."

"Oh, no," Jasmine groaned as she flopped down on her bed.

"Don't worry," Ruby said quickly. "It doesn't involve the tiara."

"I don't care," Jasmine said. "I still don't want to hear it. Don't you get it, Ruby? There's nothing we can do. I just have to drop out of the talent show—it's that simple."

"Just hear me out—*please,*" Ruby begged. "I did come all the way from another dimension, ya know. The least you can do is listen."

"All right," Jasmine conceded. "What?"

"Great," Ruby said, climbing onto Jasmine's pillow. "Okay, so while you were cleanin' up, I was thinkin' . . . all this time I've been tryin' to help you by doin' what I think the princess would do if she were here. But ya know—I'm not the princess."

Jasmine narrowed her eyes. *This* was supposed to make her feel better? "So?" she said.

"*So-o* . . . I need to stop tryin' to act like the princess and start actin' like me. I'm much better at bein' me, anyway."

"That's wonderful, Ruby," Jasmine droned, burying her face in the pillow. "I'm glad you shared that with me." *I'm doomed,* she thought. Then she felt a gentle tug on her hair. "What?" she asked, without lifting her head.

"I know it doesn't sound like much, but if I stop tryin' to help you through magic, I might actually be able to do some good. I'm usually pretty good at fixin' stuff."

Jasmine didn't move. Her life wasn't a pencil sharpener or a car engine, and she seriously doubted that Ruby could do much in the way of fixing it.

"Okay, here's a thought," Ruby said.

Jasmine turned her head so that she was facing Ruby, but she remained lying on the pillow. "What?" she asked.

"Well, I was just thinkin' about how the fabric was too expensive, and it occurred to me that when people come into the garage and they can't afford a new part for their car, we see if we can find after-market parts for them. You know, somethin' used or rebuilt, to save 'em a little cash."

"You want me to buy a used car?" Jasmine asked.

"Not a used car, wise guy," Ruby chastised. "Used *fabric.* Or maybe used clothes—you know, like that dress of Ashley's. It was cheaper than buyin' a new one, wasn't it?"

All of a sudden Jasmine sat up straight on the bed. "Ruby—you're a genius!" she exclaimed.

"I am?" Ruby asked.

"Yes! You are!" Jasmine replied. "Used clothing! That's it! That's exactly what I need. But—" Just as quickly as Jasmine's spirits had lifted, they came crashing to the ground.

"But what?" Ruby asked.

"But I still don't have enough money," Jasmine said. "Even if I could buy enough clothes for eight outfits, I probably wouldn't have any money left over to get beads or lace or buttons or fringe or any stuff to help me alter them and make them into my own designs."

"Well," Ruby said, sitting down on the pillow again and tapping her chin with her index finger. "There's gotta be a way." She and Jasmine sat there in silence for a full minute before another idea hit Ruby.

"What if folks *gave* you clothes and other stuff you could use?"

"Who's going to just give me things?" Jasmine asked.

Ruby shrugged. "Those girls you hang around with seem pretty cool—maybe they'd have some old clothes they're not usin'. Or maybe your mom. Does she ever donate clothes to thrift shops?"

Jasmine picked the tiny mechanic up in her hand and gave her a kiss on the head. "You did it again, Ruby! You really *are* a genius."

"Wow—thanks," Ruby said. Quickly Jasmine rushed out into the hall and grabbed the cordless phone from its cradle. "So . . . what are you gonna do?"

"I'm going to call Anna, Carrie, and Theresa, and I'm going to have them ask their parents if they have any old clothes—or old fabric, old curtains, old craft materials—*anything* that they want to get rid of.

About an hour later, Jasmine's doorbell started ringing, and Ruby remained sprawled on her shoulder to watch all of the merchandise arrive.

First, Anna showed up with her grandmother and a bag of fabric scraps left over from Mrs.

Lee's quilting days, a bunch of yarn, and some old jeans, khakis, and shirts that had belonged to Anna and her brother, Kim.

Carrie and her dad were next, with bags of clothes and old crafting supplies from her house, as well as Theresa's, since she was at home babysitting her younger brother.

A little later, Spence and Matt—who Anna and Carrie had called—dropped by with Matt's mom, having made a stop at Kevin's house to pick up his stuff as well. They came in carrying boxes with old curtains, unwanted bedspreads, some long strands of beads that Kevin's older sister used to have hanging over her closet door, four old green vinyl tablecloths, and three bags full of old clothes.

After they left, Jasmine and Ruby were positively giddy as they went through everything. They could almost have started their own thrift shop with all of the great stuff Jasmine's friends had donated.

By the time Sharon arrived at nearly nine o'clock, Jasmine's room was just about as cluttered with boxes and bags as it had been with sheep earlier in the day. Jasmine even considered telling Sharon that she didn't have room for anything else—until she saw the load Sharon was carrying.

"These are some dresses my grandmother bought for me that I'm never going to wear," Sharon said, handing over a cluster of hangers enclosed in plastic.

"Whoa—check out the threads!" Ruby cried, pouncing on the dresses as Jasmine hung them on the banister.

"And I had a bunch of old shoes, too. Nobody mentioned footwear, but I figured you might need some to go with all of the other stuff."

"Thanks, Sharon," Jasmine gushed, eyeing the boxful of shoes, which seemed to come in nearly as many sizes as there were shapes. "I totally forgot about shoes."

"No problem. I also have a bunch of this shiny fabric in red, orange, and yellow. My mom was going to have pillows made from it, but she never got around to it. Can you use it?"

Jasmine fingered the silky fabric. "Gabardine," she whispered. "This is perfect, Sharon!"

"Cool," Sharon said with a pleased smile. "And there's just one other bag in the car. Hold on, I'll be right back."

As Sharon ran to her father's car, Jasmine lifted the plastic off the group of hangers and gasped. There were six dresses, all in amazing fabrics, and Ruby was crawling among them.

"This is the mother lode!" the little mechanic exclaimed as she rubbed her cheek against the various fabrics. Jasmine examined the velvet, silk, chiffon, and satin designs as Ruby jumped from one dress to the next. "It's all real nice stuff—real soft and shiny, ya know? The princess would love these . . . if they were sixty sizes smaller."

"And they're all in perfect condition." Jasmine gasped, running her hand along the skirt of a beaded dress. When Sharon returned, Jasmine was holding the dresses out to her. "I can't take these," she said. "They're gorgeous. Are you sure it's okay for you to give them away?"

"Mm-hm." Sharon nodded. "I don't want them. They're too frilly. And my mom said you could do whatever you want with them—add beads, take off ribbons, cut them into pieces, whatever."

Jasmine could hardly believe her good fortune. With all of the clothes her friends had given her, and especially thanks to this last batch from Sharon, she wouldn't have to make much from scratch. Instead, she could just alter the things they'd given her, using their donated materials, and that would make meeting the talent show deadline a lot easier.

"Are you really, really sure, Sharon?"

Jasmine asked.

"Yeah, I'm sure. All of this stuff has been in the basement forever. My mom just keeps forgetting to take it to the Salvation Army."

"Wow, thanks," Jasmine said again. Then she noticed the final box Sharon had brought back from the car. "What's in there?" she asked, feeling like a child on Christmas morning.

"Oh, just some old costume jewelry—clip-on earrings, necklaces, bracelets—a bunch of stuff I used to play dress-up with when I was a kid. I think there are even a few feather boas and some hats," she added, setting the box on the floor and lifting its flaps.

"Sharon!" Jasmine exclaimed when she looked inside. The box was bursting with colorful beads, shining pearls, sparkling gems, feathers, flowered hats—more than Jasmine could ever have hoped for.

"Can you do something with all this stuff?" Sharon asked.

Jasmine's mouth dropped open. *"Can I?"* she asked. "Sharon—this is amazing. I don't even know what to say."

"You don't have to say anything," Sharon told her. "Just put together some outfits that will make Ashley Dutton realize she's a fashion *don't.*"

Jasmine laughed. "I'll do what I can."

"Good," Sharon said. "I can't stand that girl. She's such a princess."

Jasmine snuck a glance at Ruby and giggled.

"Don't go lookin' at me," Ruby said. "I'm a mechanic, remember?"

Jasmine smiled. She could barely contain her excitement. "I have so much great stuff to work with. I'm going to make sure this fashion-show is something ECS will never forget!"

CHAPTER
Nine

Jasmine worked all weekend, sketching designs based on the materials she'd received from her friends, ripping seams, and sewing things together in new arrangements. Thanks to her friends' donations, the work went quickly, and she didn't have to worry about sizes at all. She just used their old clothes as the foundations for each outfit and built from there.

Still, there was a lot of work to be done. Jasmine had been sewing so much that at one point, the sewing machine nearly gave out. Thankfully, Ruby had been there to crawl inside and give all of its parts a quick oiling, after which it had run smoothly once again.

By the time the day before the talent show rolled around, Jasmine was just about done with all of her outfits, minus a few final touches—final touches that she couldn't complete without help.

"Thank you all so much for coming over," Jasmine said to the group of friends gathered around her kitchen table. It was the first time she'd had any of them over to her house, and she was a little nervous about it. "My mom's ordering pizza for us at six, so we'll have two hours to work—if that's okay with everyone," she added, hoping that she wasn't asking too much of her new friends.

"Of course it is!" Carrie replied.

Anna licked her lips and grinned. "Mmm. I didn't know pizza was part of the deal. I'll have to call my mom and let her know I'm eating here."

"Yo—pizza's fantastic," Spence agreed, "but when do we get to see the goods?"

"Yeah," Sharon said. "Where are all the clothes?"

"Enthusiastic bunch," Ruby said from her spot on top of the toaster oven. It had been over-browning Jasmine's bagels the last few mornings, so Ruby had offered to take a look at it while Jasmine met with her friends.

Yeah, Jasmine thought. *They're enthusiastic, all right, but will they like the designs I've come up with?* She shot Ruby a nervous glance and clasped her hands to keep them from shaking.

"Get over yourself! They're gonna love your stuff!" Ruby called out. "Even *I* love your clothes, and I'm a jeans-and-overalls kind of gal, know what I mean?"

Jasmine sighed. Sure, Ruby liked her designs, but Ruby wasn't exactly normal. What if Jasmine's friends took one look at her designs and decided she was too far out there? What if they thought she was just as hopeless when it came to fashion as Ashley did? What if they discovered, through her designs, that she wasn't as conservative as she'd been pretending to be and decided that they didn't really like her?

"Enough already!" Ruby cried. "I know what you're doin' over there. You're what-iffin' yourself silly. Now cut it out, and show 'em the goods!" Ruby raised a tiny screwdriver into the air. Jasmine had found several small ones, designed for eyeglasses, at the thrift store and purchased them so Ruby could have an appropriately sized set of tools.

"Hel-lo? Earth to Jasmine," Sharon said. "Are you going to show us the clothes or what?"

Jasmine gave Ruby a small smile, then took a deep breath in and let it out slowly. "The clothes," she said, "are right out here." She shuffled into the living room and grabbed her mother's extra-large suitcase, wheeling it into the kitchen. Then she opened it and proceeded to remove several articles of clothing, which were all arranged on hangers. *Please don't think I'm a freak,* she silently pleaded, pressing her lips together.

"Wow," Carrie said as Jasmine held up one design after another.

"That's amazing," Sharon added.

Jasmine glanced over at her friends to see that all of them were smiling. And they were smiling *real* smiles, not just polite ones.

"Hey! It's my outfit!" Theresa cried, running over and touching a pair of pants with a matching top.

"No way, it's my bedspread!" Kevin said, coming over to view the same outfit.

Jasmine couldn't help but laugh. "It's both," she said. "I made the capri pants out of the old paisley-patterned bedspread Kevin's mom donated, and then I used the same fabric—along with some of the gabardine Sharon's mom gave me—to make the ruffled tank."

"I love it!" Theresa said.

"Really?" Jasmine asked.

Theresa nodded emphatically. "Yes. It's

beautiful, it's perfect, it's exactly what I wanted!"

Jasmine felt a grin stretch across her face and shot a quick glance at Ruby, who was jumping up and down on the toaster, shouting, "Told you so! Told you so!" Then she turned back to Theresa.

"Actually, there's one more piece to that outfit," Jasmine told her. She ran back to the living room and returned with a box full of accessories, among them a black velvet hat with a bright red poppy sewn on the front. "You get a lid, too."

"That hat is the best," Theresa said. Then she bit her lip. "Do you think, maybe, I could try it all on?"

"Do you really want to?" Jasmine asked.

"Are you kidding?" Theresa replied.

Jasmine giggled. "Of course you can try it on. In fact, that's exactly what I need you guys for. I mean, I do need some help adding a few things, too—a few beads and bows and stuff here and there—but really, what I need most . . . is models."

"Models?" Matt asked, his eyebrows shooting into the air.

Jasmine winced. "Yeah, models," she said. Matt didn't look thrilled with the idea, and

Jasmine began to worry that she'd gone too far.

"What do you mean, models?" Kevin asked.

"Well," Jasmine started tentatively, "I need people to try on the clothes so I can make some final alterations, but then I'm also going to need some of you to model for me in the show tomorrow night." She was scared to ask the next question, but it had to be asked. "Is anyone interested?"

"Sure, I already said I'd model," Sharon said. "I've done it before, plenty of times. And I'm really good at it."

Jasmine caught Ruby's eye and smirked.

"Spunk, I tell ya," Ruby remarked. "That girl's got spunk. I like it."

"You know, I can even show the rest of you how to walk and turn and everything," Sharon added.

"Thanks, Shar," Matt intoned. "But I've pretty much mastered walking at this point."

"Does that mean you'll model an outfit?" Anna asked.

Matt scrunched up his eyebrows. "*Me?* I thought all of the clothes were for girls."

"Nope." Jasmine shook her head. "I actually have a couple of guy outfits, too."

"Oh," Matt started, "well . . . I don't know. I—"

"Come on, Dana," Kevin said. "Don't you want to be in the show?"

"I have an outfit you can wear, too, Kev," Jasmine said.

"Me?" Kevin asked, ruffling his hair. "Oh, thanks, but—I think Matt would make a much better model."

"No way," Matt protested.

"Gentlemen, gentlemen," Spence interrupted. "Do I have to do all the work around here? I'd be happy to wear some of your fresh designs, Jasmine. What do we have—some funky cargo pants? Skater gear?"

"How about a vinyl tuxedo?" Jasmine asked, producing a complete outfit—jacket, pants, tie, and cummerbund—made out of dark green vinyl.

"Hey, those are the old tablecloths from our family picnics!" Kevin exclaimed.

Spence took one look at the tux and grabbed it. "Now, *this* is a suit," he said, eyeing the zigzag stitching along the lapels, which had been done in multicolored thread. "Where can I try it on?"

"That one's yours," Jasmine said.

"You know it!" Spence replied. "And give Kev the other guy outfit, whatever it is. If our act is after yours, we can wear the clothes for our gig, too."

"That's an awesome idea!" Jasmine said. "Will you do it, Kev?"

Kevin winced. "I guess," he said.

"Great!" Jasmine gushed. "So far, that's Sharon, Spence, and Kev. What about the rest of you?"

"Guess I'm out, huh?" Matt asked with a grin. "Aren't there only two outfits for guys?"

"Yes, but I need someone to do music," Jasmine told him.

"From backstage?" Matt asked. Jasmine nodded. "Perfect," Matt said. "I'm your guy. Just point me to the CD player."

"I'll model my outfit if you want me to, Jasmine," Theresa said.

Carrie and Anna looked at each other and nodded, and then Anna spoke up. "We can model, too—if you need us."

Jasmine smiled brightly. She couldn't believe how well things were coming together. "This is so awesome, you guys! Thank you so much!"

Just then, Spence came back out in his tux and strutted across the kitchen floor. "I'm a super fly guy / watchin' time go by / kickin' it live / in my vinyl tie."

Everyone laughed and applauded as Spence segued into an improvised break dance, which continued until Sharon clapped loudly to get everyone's attention.

"Hey, don't we have some work to do? We only have an hour and a half till pizza," she said, pointing at her watch.

"Where should we start, Jasmine?" Anna asked, and everyone else turned their attention to Jasmine as well.

"Well . . ." Jasmine didn't want to sound bossy, but her friends were definitely looking to her for direction. "I guess the first thing I need is for everyone to try on their clothes, so I can see if any alterations need to be made. I used your old clothes for most of the designs."

"This is *so* cool," Theresa said. "I feel like I'm working on a real fashion show—like the ones they show on cable."

"Yeah," Carrie agreed. "You're so good at this stuff, Jasmine. Maybe you'll really be a fashion designer someday."

Jasmine blushed. "I hope so," she said.

"And when you are, I'll be your top model," Sharon said, "when I'm in between court cases, that is. I'm going to be a lawyer, too, you know."

"Ha! You see? I told you that you didn't have anything to worry about," Ruby yelled. "They love you!"

Jasmine grinned at the little mechanic and at all of her friends. Everyone did seem really excited, and they didn't seem to have a problem with Jasmine giving them instructions, either.

"I'd be psyched to have you model for me, Sharon," Jasmine said. "In between court cases, of course." Sharon shot her a smug smile. "As I was saying, most of the outfits should fit fine as they are. The only one that might need more serious alterations is yours, Theresa. I made the pants and the top from scratch."

Theresa held the pants up to her waist and kicked one leg out to see where they fell. "They look perfect, but I'll try them on anyway."

"Great," Jasmine said. "And you know, while I'm working with one person, maybe the rest of you could help out with sewing and gluing?" Everyone nodded, and Jasmine continued. "The glue gun is on the counter and it's already hot, and there are a bunch of needles and spools of thread in that basket on the table. You should be able to tell from my drawings—right there in that sketch pad—where I need you to put sequins, ribbons, beads, and everything, but if you have any questions, just ask. Okay?"

All of Jasmine's friends agreed and got down to work without delay. Every so often, though, one of them would approach her—mostly Carrie, Anna, or Theresa—to tell her how cool her designs were and how awesome it was that they were all able to help her finish them. After a while, Jasmine stopped feeling so self-conscious and actually started to feel like a real designer preparing for a real fashion show. It was the most fun she'd had since she moved back to Newcastle and, she realized, the first time she'd really felt like herself.

When the pizza finally came, the clothes were finished, and everyone had been fitted for their outfits for the big show.

"I'm glad that's over," Kevin said as he grabbed a slice of pepperoni and took a seat at the table. "My thumb's killing me."

"Your thumb?" Sharon asked.

"Yeah—I kept stabbing myself with the needle while I was sewing on those . . . little circles."

"They're called *sequins,* Kev," Theresa told him.

"Well, whatever they are, they're impossible to sew," Kevin said, taking a bite of his pizza.

"Or maybe," Matt said, reaching for a piece

of mushroom and green pepper, "you're just not a very good sewer."

Everyone laughed except Kevin, who nearly choked on his pizza. "Hey—it's not my fault I have big hands. A lot of guys do. That's why sewing is considered women's work."

"Excuse me?" all five girls said at the same time.

Spence looked at Kevin, shook his head, and then dropped it into his hands. Matt just laughed.

"What?" Kevin said. "It's true. You have to have little hands for sewing. It helps for cooking, too. And washing dishes—all that sort of housework stuff. That's why women usually take care of those things."

"My parents split the chores," Theresa said.

"So do mine," Carrie added. "And my dad cooks more often than my mom does."

"My father sews on all his own buttons," Anna said, "and I've never heard him say anything about his hands being too big for that kind of work."

"Hey, I was just saying—" Kevin started, but Jasmine cut him off.

"I think you've already said enough, Kev," she said.

"Yeah," Sharon agreed. "If I were you, I'd

stop talking and just eat the pizza, which, by the way, came from Pie in the Sky, where Joe—a *man*—does all the cooking."

Kevin stared wide-eyed at all of his female friends, uncertain what to say. So, instead of speaking, he just took another bite of his slice.

"Whoa—careful how you hold that pizza, Kev," Spence joked. "I wouldn't want you to bite that big thumb of yours." And everyone, including Kevin, laughed.

CHAPTER Ten

Jasmine glanced at her outfit in her full-length mirror and sighed. She was wearing a pair of plain tan pants she'd borrowed from Carrie and a simple white peasant blouse that belonged to her mother.

"Hey—it's almost time to leave for the talent show," Ruby called from Jasmine's nightstand. She'd been working on Jasmine's old clock radio, trying to improve its reception. "You'd better get dressed."

Jasmine rolled her eyes. "I *am* dressed," she said.

Ruby eyed Jasmine's outfit, curling her lip with distaste. "Is that what you're wearin'?" she asked.

"I guess so," Jasmine said, turning from side to side. "What do you think?"

"I'll tell you what I think," Ruby replied. "*Blah.* That's what I think."

"What do you mean? What's wrong with it?"

"Nothin's wrong with it, exactly," Ruby said. "But there's nothin' *right* with it, either."

"What are you talking about?"

"Whaddya think I'm talkin' about? I'm talkin' about the reason you look so sad right now: it's boring!"

"Ruby!"

"Hey—you asked, I answered. That outfit is boring. Boring, boring, boring. Bland. Blah. Blech. Dull, dreary—"

"Okay, okay," Jasmine cut in. "I get the idea."

"And you agree with me, don'tcha?"

Jasmine glanced in the mirror again and frowned. "I guess," she said. "But I don't have anything else to wear."

"Are you kiddin' me?" Ruby shouted. "I was lookin' through your closet before. You have all kinds of really fun clothes. Why not wear some of those?"

Jasmine rolled her eyes. "You know why," she said. "I can't wear my own clothes. Everyone at school laughs at me when I do, especially Ashley Dutton. If I wore any of that stuff tonight, she'd laugh me right off the stage."

"But doesn't she laugh at you even when you wear boring stuff?" Ruby asked.

"I suppose," Jasmine admitted. "But it would

be ten times worse if I wasn't working so hard to blend in."

Ruby tilted her head as she contemplated Jasmine's words. "That's the thing, Jasmine," she said finally. "I don't think you were meant to blend in. Not any more than I was meant to be a princess."

Jasmine smiled. "You definitely weren't meant to be a princess," she said, eyeing Ruby's outfit. After working on the toaster oven, Ruby's dress had looked even worse than it did after her stint in the pencil sharpener. So, while Jasmine was finishing up the outfits for the talent show, she'd taken a few minutes to piece together an outfit more befitting a mechanic—blue overalls, just like the ones Ruby wore back at the garage.

"And you weren't meant to be boring," Ruby announced. Jasmine cocked her head. "This isn't boring," she said, examining her reflection in the mirror. "It's . . ." She tried to think of another word to describe her outfit, but nothing came to mind. "You're right," she admitted finally, "it's boring. Bland, blah, blech, and all that other stuff, too."

"Exactly—and you're a fashion designer," Ruby said. "So what are you doing in uninteresting, run-of-the-mill clothes?"

"Saving myself from hours of torment," Jasmine replied.

"But you're not," Ruby told her. "For one thing, you're not happy wearin' the same clothes everyone else wears—it's not your style."

"Yeah, but I'm also not happy being teased about my clothes all day long, either," Jasmine retorted.

"Have you tried wearing your own clothes?" Ruby asked.

"At ECS? Just once," Jasmine said, "and I stood out like Kevin's sore thumb."

"Standing out isn't always a bad thing."

"Well, it was when I tried it," Jasmine said.

"But it wouldn't be if you didn't pay so much attention to people like Ashley Dutton, would it?"

Jasmine sighed. "How can I *not* pay attention to her? She's constantly making fun of me," she said. "And I can't avoid her all day, every day. Plus she has friends in my class who are always giggling at me."

"Yeah, but you have friends in your class who are always standin' up for you—*and* complimentin' you, *and* tellin' you how much they like your designs. So why can't you focus on them?"

Jasmine wrinkled her nose. "Because . . . well . . . I don't know."

"See? I think *that's* the problem. You're givin' Ashley more credit than she deserves. You're lettin' what *she* thinks of you matter too much. So much that you're pretendin' to be someone you're not—just like I was."

Jasmine squinted. "What do you mean?"

"Well, the princess wasn't the only one who thought it would be fun to change places. I was kind of tired of bein' a mechanic, too."

"But I thought you *loved* being a mechanic," Jasmine said.

"Oh, I do," Ruby replied. "I love everything about it—except the way other people treat me. Ya see, most of the time, people are pretty cool, but every once in a while, someone will come along who makes me feel dumb just 'cause I like workin' on cars and gettin' all greasy. It's like they think I'm second-rate or somethin', ya know? And I guess I thought that if I was a princess, well, maybe people would give me a little more respect. But you know what I figured out?"

"What?" Jasmine asked.

"*I* didn't have any respect for myself as a princess. Not that I think there's anything wrong with wearin' nice dresses and meetin' with emperors and comin' up with policies and eatin' with the right spoon and fork all the time. It's just that, well—it's not me. I'm happiest when I'm workin' on machines, fixin' things, getting' dirty. I'm happiest when I'm myself."

"But what about the people that make you feel dumb?" Jasmine asked.

"I've decided I'm not gonna let them get me down," Ruby replied. "I know I'm not dumb, and ya know, I don't think they can make me feel dumb unless I buy into it. So, I'm not gonna. And you shouldn't, either. I think you'd be a lot happier being *yourself,* too."

"But I am being myself," Jasmine protested.

"Not really," Ruby said. "I mean, you made all those amazing clothes, which is definitely doin' something you love and doin' it your way, but now you're plannin' to get up onstage and talk about them, dressed like . . . well, look in the mirror. You're tryin' to be yourself without standin' out, and that's not gonna work. If you're gonna show off Jasmine Porter designs, you have to be Jasmine Porter—not some watered-down version of who you really are."

"I don't know, Ruby," Jasmine said. "What if Ashley and her friends show up and make fun of me? I'll get all flustered and totally mess up."

"Jasmine," Ruby said, looking straight into

her eyes. "I don't mean to make you nervous or anything, but if Ashley shows up, she's gonna make fun of you no matter what you're wearin'. So why not dress the way *you* want to dress? Don't let her break your spirit. Don't tone down your fashion style—turn it up. Show her that it doesn't matter what she thinks because guess what. It doesn't."

Jasmine checked out her reflection in the mirror again and realized just how *not her* the clothes she was wearing were. None of them even belonged to her. And although the tan pants worked well for Carrie, and the white blouse looked fine on her mom, they weren't Jasmine's style at all.

"You know something?" Jasmine said, glancing up at her tiny friend. "You're right. I'm going to wear what I want to wear. I'm tired of pretending to be something I'm not. Or is it that I've been pretending *not* to be something I *am?*" she wondered out loud.

"Huh?" Ruby asked.

"Never mind. It doesn't matter. Either way, you're right. This is *my* night, and I'm presenting *my* fashion show, and I'm going to wear *my* clothes. And if Ashley Dutton or anyone else has a problem with that . . . I'll . . . I'll . . . well, I'll do something," Jasmine finished.

"Something, huh? Yikes," Ruby teased. "But it's a start. Now get out of those boring clothes and put on somethin' fun."

Jasmine grinned and ran for her closet, realizing that for the first time in over a week, she was actually excited to get dressed.

"Whoa, Jasmine! You've really outdone yourself tonight," Ashley said just an hour later. Jasmine was headed backstage to do a final check on her designs before her act, and Ashley had caught up to her in the hall.

Currently, Kirk Goldsberry, the boy Ashley'd had such a crush on when she was in third grade, was onstage, playing guitar. He was singing "You're a Big Girl Now," by Bob Dylan, and he wasn't half bad, but apparently, Ashley didn't have a thing for him anymore. Otherwise she'd be in there watching instead of picking on Jasmine.

"What do you call that outfit anyway? Operation Fashion Disaster?" Ashley taunted.

Jasmine felt her heart speeding up, but she tried not to let on. "Look, I'm up next, Ashley. I don't have time for you right now," Jasmine told her.

"That's it! Ignore and move on," Ruby cheered from the side pocket of Jasmine's camouflage-print dress. It was a pretty standard design—a camisole-like top with a flared skirt—but Jasmine had added fake foliage in various places on the dress to give it more texture. She'd even glue-gunned a rubber snake just above the hemline in the front.

"Whatever you say, GI Jane," Ashley jeered, smirking as she went to join her giggling friends, who were waiting for her just outside the auditorium.

Once Jasmine was out of the hall and in the backstage area, she stopped walking, clenched her fists, and groaned. "Why does she have to do that?" she muttered. "I was fine before, but now my palms are all sweaty and I feel like I'm going to throw up."

"Don't let her get to you," Ruby instructed her. "Just have faith in yourself and focus on what you have to do, which is get ready for the show."

"You're right," Jasmine said. "What Ashley thinks isn't important. I just have to stay focused." She walked over to the spot where she'd hung all of her clothes, pleased to see that Carrie, Sharon, Anna, and Theresa were already in their first outfits. "You guys look great," she said, walking around each of them and giving all of their clothes a tug here and there to make sure everything hung right. "Perfect," she said, standing back to admire them.

"Everything looks great, Jazz," Theresa said. "People are going to love your designs."

I hope so, Jasmine thought. Then she walked over to check the clothes that were still hanging. "Oh, no!" she cried, noticing the hem on her favorite dress—it had come undone in one section and the ruffle was hanging down.

"What is it, Jasmine?" Carrie asked.

"Sharon's second dress," Jasmine said. "The stitching came out along the bottom and it looks terrible."

"It's not that bad," Sharon said, crouching down next to her. "Can't you just pin it?"

Jasmine shook her head. "It won't look right. We have to fix it. This is the best dress in the collection—the show won't be as good without it." Jasmine stood up and hurried over to her mother's suitcase. "I have thread and needles in here," she said. "Quick, Sharon—put on the dress and I'll sew the hem back up."

Just then, the girls heard Ms. Hamlin's voice from onstage. "Thank you, Kirk," she said as the audience finished applauding. "For our next act, we have . . ."

Jasmine stared at her friends.

"It's you, Jasmine! You have to get out there," Theresa said.

"It's okay, Jazzy. Breathe—just breathe," Ruby coached. "You have your note cards in your hand, and you're ready. Just stay calm and it'll all work out."

Jasmine listened to Ruby's voice and followed her instructions. She took a few deep breaths, regained her composure, and then glanced over at Spence and Kevin, who were just getting into their outfits.

"Yo—M.C.! Mr. Big Hands! I need you guys over here now!" she called. She'd never dared to be quite so outspoken with her friends before, but she didn't have time to second-guess herself now. Spence and Kevin hurried over to see what was going on. "The ruffle on the bottom of this dress needs to be fixed, but I have to get onstage, and the girls are modeling the first four outfits. Spence, I need you to sew, and Kevin, I need you to put on the dress so he gets it straight."

"You need . . . *what?*" Kevin asked.

"You heard me," Jasmine said.

"But . . . why can't Spence wear the dress?" Kevin asked.

"Because he sews faster than you do with

those big hands of yours. And besides, you and Sharon are the same height," Jasmine said.

"But—"

"No buts, Kevin. Just do this for me, please? It's the only way to make it work. And I'll owe you big. I'll buy you a pizza for lunch tomorrow or something, okay?"

Kevin was staring at Jasmine like he was in shock.

"Come on, Kev—you heard the lady. Don't give her stress / just put on the dress," Spence said.

"Please?" Jasmine asked.

Kevin swallowed hard, then slowly took the dress from Jasmine and stepped into it. "All right. But I want that pizza. With plenty of pepperoni. And make it a large."

"Awesome. Thanks, Kev. Thanks, Spence," Jasmine said. Then she glanced behind them. "Are you ready with the music, Matt?" she called.

Matt looked up from the CD player, caught sight of Kevin in the dress and Spence kneeling at his feet working on the ruffle, and doubled over, laughing.

"Don't laugh too hard," Jasmine told him. "You're about the same height as Theresa. If anything goes wrong with her next outfit, *you'll* be playing dress dummy."

At that, Matt straightened up. "Uh . . . nice work, Spence. Kev," he said, nodding at each of them. "I'm, uh, just going to queue the music now."

"All right," Jasmine said, grinning at all of her friends. "Let's break a leg." As she walked onto the stage, the audience applauded, but the clapping died down before she had reached the microphone, so she had to take her last few steps in silence.

"You were fabulous back there!" Ruby told her as Jasmine settled her note cards on the podium. "So confident, so in charge, so *you.* If I didn't know better, I'd think you'd been puttin' together fashion shows for years."

Jasmine blushed slightly at Ruby's words and then more deeply as she caught Ashley Dutton's eye. Ashley was in the front row with three of her friends, and all of them were smirking like crazy. For just a moment, Jasmine froze and forgot everything she was about to say.

"Don't let her get in your head, Jazz!" Ruby yelled. "It's not about her—it's about you. And you can do this. Just be yourself. *Be Jasmine Porter.*"

Jasmine breathed in deeply and glanced down at her note cards. When she looked back up again, she forced herself to avoid Ashley

Dutton's gaze. Instead she looked out at her mother, who was beaming up at her from the fifth row, and began speaking.

"Hi," she said, her voice cracking ever so slightly. Ashley Dutton and her friends were giggling, but Jasmine pulled herself together and willed herself to ignore them.

"I'm Jasmine Porter, and tonight I'm going to introduce you to a line of clothing I designed all by myself," she said, reading from her first note card. "I like to call it the Jasmine Porter Second-Time-Around Collection because every item in this line was created from secondhand clothes and fabrics that were donated to me for this show."

Again Jasmine heard Ashley and her friends snickering, and she nearly faltered. "Forget them," Ruby said. "No one else is laughin'. Everybody likes this secondhand fashion show idea—I can see it in their faces. They wanna hear more."

Jasmine cleared her throat and kept talking. "I took apart old dresses and combined their fabrics with old curtains, bedspreads, tablecloths—whatever seemed to work—and created all of the fashions you're about to see. And because my designs reuse old items in a fresh, new way," Jasmine continued, reading from another note card, "I like to think that not only is the Jasmine Porter Second-Time-Around Collection sassy and stylish, but it's also kind to the environment."

Suddenly a few people in the back of the room began to clap, and in a moment nearly the whole auditorium had joined in on a brief round of applause. "Recyclers!" Ruby yelled. "We have recyclers in the house, and they love you, Jazzy!" Ruby was so excited, she was jumping up and down on the podium. "Now show 'em your stuff!"

Jasmine turned toward the left wing of the stage and gave Matt a thumbs-up to start the music. Immediately techno beats began pumping through the auditorium, and Theresa started across the stage in her first outfit. *This is it,* Jasmine thought. *My first fashion show.*

Before she started her narration, Jasmine glanced to the wings once again to check on Spence and Kevin's progress and received a big okay sign from Kevin, who was out of the dress and back in his beachwear.

"This outfit is called 'Theresa,' and it's named after my friend Theresa, who just happens to be modeling it," Jasmine said. Theresa flashed a huge grin at the audience and waved to her family—her mom, her dad, her older sister, and her little brother—who all waved back and applauded for her.

"The flared capri pants were made from an old bedspread, which I also used to create the ruffle on the tank top," Jasmine continued. "The rest of the tank was sewn from recycled upholstery fabric donated by Katherine Ross, and the crushed velvet hat was made from an old scarf, also donated by Mrs. Ross." Theresa walked to the edge of the stage, turned a few times, and then started off. "Thank you, Theresa," Jasmine said, and the crowd applauded.

"That was awesome, Jazzy!" Ruby said. "Here comes Sharon!"

Jasmine flipped to her next card and continued narrating. "This dress that Sharon is wearing is called 'Ruby.'"

"You named one after me?!" the little mechanic shouted, clasping her hands over her heart.

Jasmine grinned—she had known Ruby would be pleased—but she didn't miss a beat. "The 'Ruby' is for the girl who wants a dress that's elegant but functional. It features side pockets large enough to store money, keys, lip balm, or even a small screwdriver, but it remains elegant, thanks to its soft lines and beadwork."

"You're not gonna believe it, Jazzy, but they're smiling!" Ruby shouted suddenly. "Ashley's friends are smiling. They're enjoyin' your show!"

Jasmine darted a quick look toward the front row and saw that all of the girls sitting with Ashley were indeed leaning forward and paying close attention. Ashley, on the other hand, was sulking, her arms folded across her chest.

"Thank you, Sharon," Jasmine said as Sharon walked offstage, and this time the applause from the audience was even louder.

"This is goin' great!" Ruby cried, but Jasmine didn't need to be told—she could feel how well things were going. Her hands were still a bit shaky, but it was more from excitement now than anxiety. And although it was nice to see that Ashley had been silenced—at least temporarily—Jasmine was aware that what she was enjoying the most was being able to express her creativity to all of these people. Of course, it helped that everyone seemed to like them, but the best part was that she was finally being true to herself. She was wearing one of her favorite dresses, without embarrassment and showing people who she really was, without censoring herself.

And now, possibly because Jasmine was

enjoying her show so much, the crowd seemed to be getting into it, too. The music was pumping, and a few girls in the back of the auditorium had started dancing. Some members of the audience were swaying in their seats and others were even clapping to the beat.

While she was waiting for Carrie to start out, Jasmine glanced down at Ashley Dutton one more time and almost felt bad for her. Ashley was positively pouting while her friends were all smiling and eagerly awaiting the next outfit. And that's when Jasmine realized that even if Ashley had been making fun of her at that moment, it wouldn't have mattered. Jasmine was feeling so good about herself and her accomplishments that an entire army of Ashley Duttons couldn't have brought her down.

CHAPTER Eleven

"Congratulations, guys!" Jasmine called as Spence and Kev returned from the stage with their Best Musical Performance award.

"What did you get?" Carrie asked.

Spence waved an envelope in the air. "Gift certificates to Sound Factory," he said. "Kev and I will be livin' it up, picking out some new beats this weekend."

"And then I'm going to be having free pizza, right, Jasmine?" Kevin asked.

"Absolutely," Jasmine said with a grin.

"Yo, Carrie and Sharon," Spence said, "I just want to thank you ladies for not entering the show. If either one of you had, Kev and I would have had some serious competition up there."

"I don't know about that," Carrie said. "You guys were pretty good. I'm not sure I would have measured up even if I had come up with a song."

"Why didn't you sing, Sharon?" Theresa asked. "I thought you had a song picked out and everything."

"I did," Sharon said with a shrug. "But then my voice teacher scheduled a recital for this weekend, so I decided to save my voice for that and just focus on my modeling talent for tonight."

Jasmine smiled. "And you were awesome, Sharon. You were all awesome," she added, gazing at her friends. "Thank you so much for helping me out. I couldn't have done it without you."

"It's so great that you won the Most Unique Talent award," Theresa said, grinning from ear to ear.

"Yeah," Carrie said. "It's so perfect! You totally deserved it!"

All of the others nodded in agreement, and Spence put his hand up for a high five. "Way to go, Jazzy P.," he said as she slapped his palm.

"Thanks, but I think it was your dancing that won it for me, Spence. The crowd went wild when you started breakin' it down."

"I do what I can," Spence said with a grin, and everyone laughed.

Meanwhile, Jasmine looked down at the gift certificate in her hand that entitled her to a mini shopping-spree at Craft Mania, the fabric store in the mall.

After chatting about the show a little more and making plans to meet at the mall the next day, Spence, Kevin, Matt, and Sharon headed out, while Jasmine, Carrie, Anna, and Theresa headed backstage to pack up all the clothing and accessories so that Jasmine could take them home and get them cleaned.

They were just about finished loading everything into Mrs. Porter's suitcase when they were interrupted.

"Jasmine?"

All four girls whirled around, surprised to see Ashley Dutton standing right there.

Jasmine rolled her eyes. "Look, Ashley," she said. "I'm sure that whatever you came to say to me can wait until Monday morning. I've had a really good night so far, and I'm planning to have a great weekend, so I don't need you to spoil any of it."

Ashley smiled smugly, and it seemed pretty clear that she wasn't willing to wait three days to insult Jasmine. "Secondhand fashions?" she sneered. "Did you really think—?" But before Ashley could finish her sentence, Heather

Towne—the most popular girl in the eighth grade—rushed over with a few of her friends.

"It's Jasmine, right?" she said, walking straight past Ashley without even acknowledging her.

Jasmine glanced at her friends nervously, wondering if she was about to be harassed by someone even more popular than Ashley. "Um . . . yeah?"

Heather grinned broadly. "I just wanted to tell you that we all *loved* your fashion show," she said. She looked around at her friends, who all nodded and smiled at Jasmine, too. Suddenly Jasmine felt like some kind of celebrity.

"Really?" she asked.

"Absolutely," Heather said. "And that dress you're wearing is amazing! I'm really surprised that I haven't seen you around school before now. You have such unique, funky clothes, it seems like you would stand out."

"Well," Jasmine hesitated, "I guess I haven't really been wearing any of my original stuff lately."

"Why not?" Heather asked. "It's so cool!"

Jasmine glanced at Ashley, who was definitely avoiding her gaze. "Uh, I'm not sure," Jasmine said, "but from now on, I think I'll be wearing a lot more of it."

"Awesome," Heather replied. "I can't wait to see your outfit on Monday morning."

Jasmine's face lit up. Less than two weeks ago she'd been trying to avoid standing out, but now she was looking forward to it.

"So, anyway," Heather went on. "After seeing all of your cool designs tonight, I was wondering—do you think you could design a dress for me for the spring formal? I'd buy all of the materials and pay you and everything, of course, but I'd want you to do something like what you did for your show—you know, take secondhand stuff and turn it into something new. That's a really cool idea."

"I—"

"I loved it, too," Molly Leding said. "And I was hoping you could make me a dress for the formal, too. And I want you to make my boyfriend, Mike, a suit like the one that kid was wearing—the one who raps all the time."

Jasmine glanced at her friends, who were all positively beaming. "Wow," she said, turning back to Heather and Molly and the others. "Thanks, you guys. I mean, I'm so glad you liked my designs." *My designs,* Jasmine thought. Just saying it sounded cool.

"So can you do it?" Heather asked.

"Uh . . . yeah, I guess," Jasmine said with a shrug. "I mean, I can try."

"Awesome!" Heather said. "Here's my phone number. The dance isn't for another six weeks, but maybe we can get together this weekend so I can kind of tell you what I'm looking for, okay?"

"Okay," Jasmine said, taking the slip of paper from Heather's hand.

"Cool. Give me a call," Heather said. Then she, Molly, and the others turned to go. "Oh, hi, Ashley," Heather said on her way out the door. Ashley had practically backed out of the room while Heather and Molly had arrived. "I was so excited about Jasmine's clothes, I didn't even see you before. If you came back to get her to design a dress for you for the Spring Fling, you'll have to wait. She's doing mine first."

Jasmine watched as Ashley shifted from one foot to the other awkwardly. It was nice to see her squirm.

"Oh. Darn," Ashley said, trying to look disappointed. "Well, I guess I'll just have to get in line."

"You better catch her now," Heather said. "I have a feeling she's going to get mobbed on Monday." And with that, Heather and her friends exited. Once they were gone, Ashley looked back at Jasmine and scowled.

"So, Ashley," Jasmine started, "what was it you were saying before Heather came in? Something about *secondhand fashions* and 'did I really think—'? Think what?" Jasmine asked.

Ashley stared for a moment, pressing her lips together and eyeing Jasmine, Carrie, Theresa, and Anna. "Actually," she said after a moment, "I just came back to say that I thought you did a nice job." And with that, Ashley skulked out the door.

"Thanks," Jasmine called after her. Then she turned to her friends.

"That was incredible, Jasmine!" Theresa said.

"I guess she won't be bugging you anymore," Carrie added.

"Way to go, Jasmine," Anna said.

Jasmine grinned. *And all I had to do was have faith in myself,* she thought, remembering Ruby's words. *Ruby!*

"I'll be right back," Jasmine told her friends. "I left all my notes on the mike stand." In truth, she'd left Ruby there when the little fix-it queen had begged Jasmine to let her take a look inside the microphone—it had been breaking out periodically during the last act, and Ruby was sure she could fix it.

"Ruby!" she hissed. "Ruby—we did it! Ashley Dutton is never going to bother me again! Did you hear that, Ruby? We—" Jasmine stopped short when she reached the podium and saw not her little mechanic friend, but instead the silver princess button she'd originally ripped off her purple dress.

"Oh, no, Ruby," she said, picking up the button and holding it close to her heart. Jasmine took a deep breath and let it out slowly. "I guess I knew you wouldn't be here forever," she whispered. "But I miss you already," she added. "I bet the garage is glad to have their best mechanic back, though."

Jasmine took another look at the button and realized that something was different about it now. Instead of having a loop on the back so that it could be sewn onto an article of clothing, the button now had a loop at the top with a small silver ring through it. In fact, it didn't look like a button at all—it looked like a charm.

Remembering the bracelet that Theresa, Carrie, and Anna had given her—the one she'd been wearing nonstop since her first day at ECS and the one that had definitely brought her plenty of good luck—Jasmine reached down, unclasped it, and added Ruby to the chain. Then she refastened the bracelet around her wrist and admired it. That's when she noticed that there was something inscribed on the back of the princess charm she'd just attached. Jasmine flipped the charm over and read the tiny writing:

Be yourself—and never wear a formal gown to fix a toaster oven.

Jasmine chuckled. "I hope the princess isn't too upset about that," she said quietly. "And yes, I'm definitely going to be myself from now on," she added. "Thanks, Ruby." Then she looked at the other charms on the bracelet and smiled. "And thanks to the rest of you, too. Whoever you are."